William James Currie

Lays and Lyrics

William James Currie

Lays and Lyrics

ISBN/EAN: 9783744769112

Printed in Europe, USA, Canada, Australia, Japan

Cover: Foto ©Andreas Hilbeck / pixelio.de

More available books at **www.hansebooks.com**

LAYS AND LYRICS

BY

WILLIAM JAMES CURRIE

AUTHOR OF "DORIC LILTS."

GALASHIELS

PRINTED BY JOHN M'QUEEN

MDCCCXCI

———————

" These straggling thoughts, whilst passing through the mind,
  Burst forth in verse, unpolished, unrefined ;
  But should they strike one sympathetic strain
  In any heart, I've labour'd not in vain."

JAMES CURRIE.

CONTENTS.

INTRODUCTORY.

By what some assert to be a " Divine right " princes claim the power to follow in the footsteps of their fathers, to wear the crown, and hold the sceptre of kingship. In much the same spirit the author of these pages might lay claim to bear the harp and grasp the pen, because in childhood's home the power and influence of poesy was felt and owned by a father in whose heart the minstrelsy of Burns, our national Bard, had something to do with the waking of the song-spirit.

As memory looks backwards over the past to those early days, when he eagerly watched the ready pen setting forth the poetic numbers of that true and fearless heart, fearless alike on Crimean battlefields as in the use of the pen, the author is reminded it was then arose within his own bosom the desire that he might be enabled to follow in his father's footsteps, "and sing a sang at least."

Born amid the rich beauties which Nature has so kindly gifted to the Vale of Ettrick, loved Ettrick ! famous in story, and with events chronicled in ballad, it was there the spirit of song took possession of the author's being, and led him to tread the rhymers' path, and still leads him to sing in the joy of summer time, or mid the dreary gloom of winter we...

In days of gladness, in hours of sadness song has come to heighten joy or soothe griefs, and assist in breaking the spell that is apt to fall upon and twine around the careworn heart, making life—

" Burden'd with weariness,
Bitter with dreariness."

Written by a son of toil when the labours of the day were past, these verses are without any pretension to learning or elaborate study, and they are presented to the reader as leisure hour play-things of fancy, soul-longings after truth and right, and heart-throbbings against aught that would seek to oppress our common humanity. With pleasure the author accords to his subscribers his warmest thanks for the kindly support given, enabling him for the second time to place the offerings of his Muse upon the altar of public criticism. That they may find something within these pages to beguile the otherwise weary hour, or touch a kindred chord within their breasts is the desire of

THE AUTHOR.

November 1891.

LAYS AND LYRICS.

THE MINSTREL'S RAID.

A HOLIDAY LAY.

Hail! Ettrick, thou my native vale,
Where, teeming on the mountain gale,
Come bold romance and stirring song
That pleasures well the list'ning throng.
How oft beside thy hill-born stream
I've rov'd entranced in some sweet dream
While fancy peopled once again
With chief and clansmen, hill and plain.

Then fearless rode the bold Buccleuch,
Or Murray brave, the loved, the true—
Ho! Southerns, guard your castles well,
What may befall them, who can tell,
When moonbeams kiss the hill-sides grey
And Ettrick's chieftains seek the fray,
For hearts like theirs they know not fear
Their prize to win, nor life hold dear.

B

Or, hush ! upon the breeze so calm
There surely swells King David's psalm,
Or pleading voice of earnest prayer
To Him, the God of earth and air,
That His eternal power shall wake
And all the clouds of darkness break ;
Or warning voice doth loud proclaim
The glories of the Lord's own name.

Lov'd Ettrick, by thy flowing stream
Sweet fancy leads the mystic dream,
And changing years thy beauties still
Each native heart must warmly thrill,
And oft' will wake the humble song
The whisp'ring winds shall bear along,
For lo ! a harp I found in thee—
A soldier sire gifted me.

Then wake, dear harp of Ettrick, wake,
Ring forth your notes o'er hill and brake ;
Be like the wild bird's cheering lay,
Sweet at the morn or gloaming grey.
Be to this oft sad heart of mine   ·
A source of joy with love divine ;
Lead me to sing—the stirring strain
Bids care depart and dreary pain.

Come like a breath of vernal May,
When beauty blooms in robes so gay ;
Join with the thousand thousand lays
That sound o'er Ettrick's hills and braes.

Recall again sweet boyhood's years—
The lightsome games, the joys and fears,
Known in the ancient burgh town,
The Souter's pride of old renown.

SCHULE DAYS IN SELKIRK.

AIR—" Lang, Langsyne."

Oh, the merry, merry days,
When we ran owre hills an' braes,
Heedless o' Time's rapid flight,
'Tween the dawnin' an' the nicht,
If but by the dear lo'ed bed
O' the Ettrick, roarin' red,
  We could roam in life's fair sunny mornin'.

An' I mind ' The Piper's Puil,'
Where, as truants frae the schule,
Wi' a lump o' string an' preen,
Like true fishers we'd be seen ;
Then we faund we'd broke the laws,
When we got the cane or tawse,
  Till we grat wi' the pain in the mornin'.

Hoo we'd play at "hunt the hare "—
Oh ! oor fun was grand an' rare ;
Up the Kirk Wynd we wad flee,
Doon the Back Raw sune were we :
Or up the Loan we'd gang,
Where the lovers we'd meet thrang,
  As we ran in oor games in life's mornin'

Though we lo'ed the simmer 'oors
Wi' their bonnie scented flo'ers,
Yet cauld winter, wi' its snaw,
Brocht sweet pleasures to us a' :
Doon the Brig Road we wad gang,
Where the sclyin' aye was thrang—
    What happy bairns were we in life's mornin'.

Oh ! bricht bairnhood's days lang gane—
Fu' o' pleasures a' their ain :
Fond Mem'ry, on her track,
In sweet fancy brings them back,
An' we seem to hear ilk lauch
As we ran 'boot Philiphaugh,
    Where we first saw the schule in life's mornin'.

Where are a' oor schulemates noo,
That for a' oor tiffs we'd lo'e ?
Some yet bide in oor auld toon,
Ithers scattered up an' doon.
Tho' the feck by Death's been ta'en,
We a' shall meet again
    When the Maister ca's us up on His mornin'.

————

Rude harp, we touch each trembling string,
And thus to thee we gladly sing—
Wake 'mid the rare, the beauteous scene,
The fairest of our land, I ween,
That e'er has met the minstrel's gaze,
Since first he roved in youthful days.

A gem in Nature's lap it lies,
We deign, dear harp, to say we prize :
Our heart to it still loving clings,
Responsive to the spell it flings
Round us, since childhood's early years,
We watched the swans, and stately deers.

High o'er the lake we seem'd to hear
A myriad voices sounding clear,
Sweet borne upon the sighing breeze
From flowerets rare, and verdant trees ;
The hills re-echoed back the song
That through the vale was passed along,
Till, fill'd with awe, I could not move,
Though all seem'd wrapp'd around with love,
And every voice essayed to sing—
" Come, worship Heaven's Eternal King."

How strange indeed the wond'rous spell
That wrapp'd the youthful spirit well :
'Tis even now upon the ear,
Swift borne across the lake so clear,
As, standing in my manhood's prime,
I dream of that bright golden time
When I would roam those woodlands rare,
And cull God's flow'r-gems, pure and fair.

THE HAINING—IN SIMMER.
AIR—" Rothesay Bay."

Its bonnie in the simmer :
  Gin ye will gang wi' me
The richness o' the Haining
  Wi' your ain een to see.

I wadna gie its beauty
   For a' the gowd folk hae,
While Ettrick sings sae merrily
   In its ain dear lo'ed way.

The birds are sweetly singin'
   Rich sangs that thrill the heart,
They drive awa' a' dule an' care,
   An' joyous feelin's start.
When the brume an' whins are yellow—
   My heart weel lo'es them sae—
Through The Haining I will gang
   To spend ae blythsome day.

The hills are a' sae bonnie,
   The trees are clad wi' green,
And the lake, where swans swim gracefu',
   It glows wi' gowden sheen.
An' the bosom thrills wi' pleasure
   As we spend ae lang day
'Mang God's sweet gift o' grandeur,
   Where the heart sae fain wad stay.

———

But come each wand'ring, fickle string,
And with yon am'rous blackbird sing ;
Nor wake alone your simple lays
To rich hued fragrant Nature's praise.
As calm and peaceful eve comes on,
The heart, the mind, will turn to one
We'd meet beneath the ancient elm,
And pledge to rove through love's dear realm.

Ah, Love! that binds with wond'rous chain,
We would not say your spells are vain:
A smiling face, a beaming eye,
A gentle look, the band will tie,
That holds the heart in loving thrall,
And makes some maid life's golden "all:'
Then wake, my harp; no longer sleep;
Sing the tryst one faithful heart will keep.

MY AIN DEARIE, O.

When owre the hills the sun has gane,
　　And trystin' time is here, my Jo,
I'll meet thee 'neath the spreadin' elm
　　Where Ettrick rins sae clear, my Jo;
And there beneath the shelt'rin' boughs
　　I'll woo thee, blythe and cheerie, O:
When nestlin' in my shepherd plaid,
　　Oor hearts will ne'er grow weary, O.

Nae title hie nor wealth o' gowd
　　Shall win my heart frae thee, my Jo;
For what is wealth without the love
　　That charms the heart and e'e, my Jo.
E'en let the spitefu' jibe and jeer,
　　Ne'er let their actions fear ye, O;
For while the life-blood warms my veins
　　I'll loe thee, my ain dearie, O.

The laird wha dwells in yonder ha'
   Nae joy can feel like me, my Jo ;
Though he has wealth and acres braid
   Nae lass his bride will be, my Jo.
But bliss is mine, for I hae thee,
   Sae how can I be eerie, O ;
While ilka smile e'en seems to say—
   " I'll ever be your dearie, O.'

The gowans deck the Ettrick's banks,
   The broom blooms rich an' rare, my Jo ;
Sae when the hush o' gloamin' fa's,
   O haste my plaid to share, my Jo ;
And when thou'rt clasp'd close to my heart
   Nae twa will be mair cheerie, O,
For mair than wealth or fame to me
   Is my ain bonnie dearie, O.

———

Still, harp of Ettrick, once again
I'd wake your chords in stirring strain ;
And this my parting song would be—
My native land, the grand, the free ;
Proud of the land which gave me birth—
The noblest of all lands on earth ;
It's poorest spot is rich to me,
Whilst 'tis the home of liberty.

Is there a craven foe of thine
That dares molest this home of mine ?
Let them beware, we brook no foe
Would devastate our land with woe ;

From every mountain, every vale
Would speed the men who never fail—
The tried, the trusted, and the true,
Who'd fearless dare, and nobly do,
That heaven's gift would Scotland's ever be—
The glorious right of liberty.

For Wallace, brave and kingly knight,
Who trod our vales in warlike might,
Undaunted by the southern's pride,
Oft turn'd the battle's surging tide,
Till Freedom found a lasting rest
Within each patriot Scottish breast.
Oh, knight, most true, thy worth, thy name
Shall never fade from deathless fame ;
Such deeds as thine have nerved the brave
To dare the foe, that they might save
That land whose skies shall ever be
The bright blue dome that crowns the free.

DEAR SCOTLAND, MY HOME-LAND.

Hail Scotland ! the land of green glens and mountains,
   Where liberty's banners wave fair o'er the free ;
All hail to thy forests and bright flashing fountains,
   No land bears a grandeur so dear unto me.

Hail Scotland ! rare land of the heath-bell and river,
   Our hearts' best affections around Thee shall twine,
While forest trees wave in the breeze of life's Giver,
   And songs of the song birds in summer are thine.

Proud, proud of the thistle, to guard it we'd perish,
   Sink glad to our grave 'neath the waving blue-bell;
Ah! soulless must he be whose heart cannot cherish
   The land of the mountain, the moor, and the dell.

Yes, proudly I've trod 'mongst the bright purple heather,
   And knelt where the clangour of battle has rung,
Where for freedom and truth the fearless would gather,
   And the praise of our God in true fervour was sung.

No dreamings of wealth o'er the deep heaving ocean
   Shall draw me away in some far land to pine;
Oh, no! thou possessest my warmest devotion,
   Brave Scotland, my home-land, for aye thou art mine.

Dear Scotland, my country, rare, rare is thy beauty,
   When Nature's rich grandeur around us we see;
Thy sons, ever ready, shall answer to duty,
   Though press'd by bold foemen, unconquered they'll be.

Rest now, my harp, your task is done,
Rest with the golden setting sun,
Till crown'd with love and sympathy—
More dear than wealth or fame to me.
Be this your joy to wake each string,
The weary heart from cares to bring:
Teach me the bliss of brighter spheres,
Where grief ne'er stings, nor eyes know tears.

Good night, dear vale, the minstrel sighs,
  No place like thee his heart will prize:
Sing on, lov'd Ettrick, sweet your song,
  As to the Tweed you roll along;
Good night, rare town, my birth-place true,
  And friends I love, once more adieu !
While life shall last, where'er I stray,
  My heart shall love this holiday.

MAN WAS NOT MADE TO MOURN.

(A LAY TO MY FELLOW TOILERS.)

What voice is this which speaks to me,
   Borne on each passing wind
From mountain top and restless sea ?
   'Tis pressed upon my mind.
The solemn truth of God's own word
   So many thousands spurn ;
Go, learn it from our loving Lord—
   Man was not made to mourn.

See, Nature wakes with gentle spring,
   Her beauties to disclose,
While sweet the warbling minstrels sing
   Ere they must seek repose.
How rich they breathe this lesson still
   Through trees or waving corn,
Though we should weep 'tis not God's will—
   Man was not made to mourn.

Yon poor frail wreck of womankind,
   Once pure and bright and fair,
To every sense of honour blind,
   Sunk deep in woeful care,
Was not ordained to be a blight
   'Mid all that's noble born :
'Tis taught by Him of Love and Might—
   Man was not made to mourn.

And man, with cursings deep and wild,
   While sinful passions glow,
May sink the pure and stainless child
   In dark, unhallowed woe,
Yet shall he learn as ages roll,
   Though he the truth may scorn,
Bliss is the birthright of the soul—
   Man was not made to mourn.

The curse of earth to me seems this :
   Man holdeth man in thrall,
Till, robb'd of every hope of bliss,
   In dark despair he fall.
Yet tho' the human soul is sear'd,
   The heart oft crush'd and torn,
Tho' God's own truth is curs'd and jeer'd—
   Man was not made to mourn.

Too true, oppression's hateful pow'r
   By toil-worn wights is felt ;
From early morn to latest hour
   The law of gold is dealt :
" Your time, 'tis ours, 'tis not your own,"
   Makes weary hearts forlorn.
Nor yet by such God's law is shown—
   Man was not made to mourn.

Who would not know the golden age
   By prophet bards foretold,
When love shall reign, nor greed shall wage
   It's merc'less fight for gold ?

Wake ye your songs, your chains shall break
   And peace the earth adorn,
Then love shall heal those hearts that ache—
   Man was not made to mourn.

Oh, how we gaze with longing eyes
   Across the hills of time,
To catch the dawning in the skies,
   And angel songs sublime !
They come ! They come ! and surely we
   May hail their glad return,
Proclaiming Eden's joys so free—
   Man was not made to mourn.

TO MY POET FAITHER.

A song to thee I gladly bring,
Who taught my youthful heart to sing,
             My sire.

Though sair an' hard the fecht has been
   To climb life's weary brae,
Some blinks o' joy hae whiles been oors
   To cheer us on the way.
Sae keep your heart abune life's cares
   An' trust oor Faither still—
We never dee'd in winter yet
   An' maybe never will.

In a' the saxty years ye've seen
   Swift gane ayont reca',
E'en when 'mid war's wild bluidy wark
   Your airm was shot awa',
Cam' there nae voice, nor thochts o' hame
   Your manly heart to thrill—
We never dee'd in winter yet,
   An' maybe never will.

'Twas then the pibroch's shrillest note
  · Proclaimed o'er Crimean fields—
Let Russia's hordes try a' they can,
   " A Cameron never yields."
An' weel 'twas prov'd they fand it oot,
   Sic truths bauld hearts could fill—
We never dee'd in winter yet,
   An' maybe never will.

Look back to days when we were bairns,
   An' struggles unco sair,
For ilka mou' had breid to get,
   Though whiles ye scarce kent where ;
Ye never failed, but wrocht an' sang—
   Sic times I mind them still—
We never dee'd in winter yet,
   An' maybe never will.

I mind when in oor ain auld toon,
   Dear to your heart an' mine,
Nae ane could daunt, be wha they micht,
   That fearless heart o' thine ;

Your cuttin' sang ilk tyrant fear'd,
    Wha sneakin' clamb life's hill—
We never dee'd in winter yet,
    An' maybe never will.

The langsome years hae fleetly sped,
    Your son an' dochters twa
Hae hames an' bairnies o' their ain,
    An' cares aboot them fa';
Yet aye they lo'e the auld hearthstane,
    Nor time that love can kill—
We never dee'd in winter yet,
    An' maybe never will.

Losh! faither, though its nearly white,
    Your ance broon curly hair,
An' that bronchitis mak's ye frail
    Wi' coughin' fell an' sair:
Keep up your heart an' trust oor King
    Wha saves frae ilka ill—
We never dee'd in winter yet,
    An' maybe never will.

Yet true it is that changes come,
    The dearest lo'ed maun pairt,
Let's thankfu' be through love sae great
    We a' can gang ae airt;
An' ilk dark clud is pierced wi' licht,
    This joy oor hearts to fill—
We never dee'd in winter yet,
    An' maybe never will.

SELKIRK AND FLODDEN.

[Looking over the second volume of T. Craig-Brown's " History of Selkirkshire," I made the following extract regarding Selkirk and the battle of Flodden, which was fought on September 9th, 1513 :—" From the 22nd August till the 25th October there is no entry in the burgh records, nor is the battle once alluded to, even indirectly, in the subsequent minutes. It would seem as if a silent oath had been taken that the dreadful day should be blotted for ever out of record." But to the oral traditions of old families in the burgh we are indebted for the knowledge we possess of the fact that the men of Selkirk did their duty on that disastrous day, when the flowers of Scottish chivalry were all wede away. With a little of the rhymer's license we give the story in verse.]

Three times was the pyot heard late in the e'en,
Three times the deid-licht by the same anes was seen,
While lood-flappin' shutters frichten'd mony to tears,
And strange dreamin's o' war fill'd the timid wi' fears
O waesome and weary the faither's sad moan,
" This life will be worthless," the mother's lood groan,
" Gin oor ain gallant sons hear the dule o' war's ca',"
For the Flo'ers o' the Forest micht sune wede awa'.

Oft, oft have oor lads in the battle-front been,
Where prood southern lords on their war-steeds were seen ;
Wha crafty wad steal at the grey dawn o' day,
Like the savage blood-hounds seekin' far for their prey ;
And little was heard till forth leapt the red flame,
And spear and bows seen where ance stood their loved
    hame ;
Ne'er wonder that hate grew to life in them a',
But the Flo'ers o' the Forest may sune wede awa'.

C

Frae the King cam' the summons bade the lads mount an'
    ride
To meet wi' the foe in the battle's red tide
(For the Souters o' Selkirk the King coonted leal),
And foes to the Border bows deathwards maun reel.
Frae the Peel Gait they cam', and the Water Raw, too ;
Frae the east gait and wast gait cam' Souter lads true.
O, Ettrick's wild winds, could ye no loodly blaw—
" The Flo'ers o' the Forest will sune wede awa' ?"

The burghers they met, and the summons was read,
And the joy o' the joyous how quickly it fled
When the roll it was ca'd, and ilk ane answered prood—
" The foe to the worms we shall gi'e for their food."
The aged then blessed them, their charges were gi'en,
The band in war gear mairch'd awa' doon the Green.
Through the Haining's fair wuds the sighin' winds blaw—
" O, the Flo'ers o' the Forest will sune wede awa'."

O, days lang an' drear, seemin' endless ilk nicht,
Slow, slow on Time's wings was their wearisome flicht ;
O, deep sighs that rise frae the sair-sadden'd breast,
O, tears that will fa' when in sleep they should rest ;
Low sighin', they moaned—" Will there nane ever bring
Gude news o' oor lads and oor ain noble King ?"
Could they no' hear the voice in the winds roond them fa'—
" The Flo'ers o' the Forest are a' wede awa' ?"

Sae dowie and lanesome the lassies a' greet,
The mothers speak nane when the lassies they meet,
While the grey lyart heids bend fu' low in their grief,
And life seem'd as sear'd as the autumn's red leaf.

At last, dule and weary, there rade doon the Loan
A remnant frae Flodden, heart-sair was their moan
Owre their gallant King slain, and the best o' them a'—
The Flo'ers o' the Forest were a' wede awa'.

Frae the Well o' St Mungo to the loch side there's nane
But wail for the lov'd anes that sleep mang the slain ;
The ports are unguarded, for the warders are auld,
And the lyart maun mourn their brave sons lyin' cauld.
O, Flodden, dark Flodden, oor glory is gane,
For the pride o' oor hearts lies still wi' the slain ;
And Ettrick, lane Ettrick, its rude winds may blaw-—
The Flo'ers o' the Forest are a' wede awa'.

A' the braw yellow craps maun lie waste on the lea,
And the rich, ripe fruits still maun hing on the tree,
For there's nane to use the gude sickle fu' keen ;
And the lassies meet nane wi' sweet mirth at the e'en.
The kye at the pasture a' wander at will,
And the sheep a' gae wild on the clud-crested hill ;
There's sabbin' and sighin' in cot and in ha',
For the Flo'ers o' the Forest are a wede awa.'

BRING ME FLOWERS, BEAUTIFUL FLOWERS.

Bring me flowers, beautiful flowers,
From garden trim or meadow fair,
Oh linger not, but haste and bring
Loved flowers to brighten hours of care;
Rare as thine own eyes, glancing bright,
Pure as the smile which wreathes thy lips,
Weaving a spell of mystic power
Sweet as the nectar the wild bee sips;
    Bring me flowers, beautiful flowers.

Bring me flowers, beautiful flowers,
Meet emblems all of purest love,
Bringing a calm, a peaceful rest,
That speaks of those sweet joys above.
Who can resist their wondrous charms
Subtly felt 'mid the world's stern strife,
Coming as love-gifts sent from God
To brighten and beautify life?
    Bring me flowers, beautiful flowers.

Bring me flowers, beautiful flowers,
Rich in their shades of red and blue,
Bright crimson tipp'd, lilac, and white,
Fresh with the kiss of morning dew.
I love the flowers, soul-thrilling flowers,
Free from the world's coquetting art,
They weave a powerful, holy spell
Ever around each loving heart;
    Bring me flowers, beautiful flowers.

Bring me flowers, beautiful flowers,
Kiss'd by the sun's bright golden beams,
Laughing beauties, tenderly train'd
Or blooming by wild mountain streams ;
Only bring to my longing heart
Those dear loved soul-thrilling flowers,
Though all too soon they wither and fade
In the ever fast-fleeting hours ;
Bring me flowers, beautiful flowers.

BRUSH THE COBWEBS O' CARE AWA'.

Eh ! sirce me ! but it's douf an' dreary,
The wecht o' this warl's cauld care ;
It stoiters the step that's fu' steady,
An' whitens the ance black hair.
An' the sair lane heart langs for the love
That shares the sharp sting o' pain,
An' will brush the cobwebs frae the heart
Till a' feel lichtsome again.

See yonder puir body sae thoweless—
How sad is his ance bricht e'e ;
Fu' licht he has tripped wi' his dearie,
Far ower the daisy-deck'd lea.
He steps doon life's brae unco slowly,
Thinkin' earth's joys are a' vain :
Let us brush the cobwebs frae his heart,
Till he feels lichtsome again.

An' yon lass wha was blithe as the birds,
    Liltin' awa' owre the braes,
Scarce sings ava, an' she sighs sae sair
    Through the warl's dreich dreary ways :
The siller glint frae her bonnie een,
    The blush frae her cheeks are ta'en —
Let us brush the cobwebs frae her heart
    Till she feels lichtsome again.

Losh ! arena' we selfish an' donnert,
    An' scarce worth an auld bawbee,
Keepin' sympathy a' to oorsel's
    When wae a' roond us we see.
Let us act as we'd hae ithers act,
    E'en be they auld folk or wean :
Let us brush the cobwebs frae ilk heart
    Till a' feel lichtsome again.

STARVED!

Into a house wretched and old,
Into an attic cheerless and cold,
There at the close of a winter's day,
An infant life was ebbing away—
A little maid of summers two,
With nut-brown hair and eyes of blue.

Ah ! who can paint the anguish wild
Of her who loved the dying child ?
A mother's hopes, a mother's fears,
Were bathed that night in bitter tears.
"O God !" she cried, " and can it be
My darling babe must go from me ?
Shall cruel Death claim thee its own,
And I be left, dear one, alone ? "

Up in that little attic room,
Shadows twisting out of the gloom,
Feeble the lamp's poor flickering ray
Fell on the babe passing away,
Fell on the beautiful nut-brown hair,
Fell on the blue eyes' vacant stare.
Mother, thy babe is dying fast,
Pain and sorrow soon shall be past.

Kneeling beside the pallet there,
Feeling the pangs of black despair,
She prays, " Oh spare my darling child."
She starts, can it be her babe has smiled ?
Yes, smiled, and then, alas ! she's dead,
One more starved through lack of bread,
Starved, O God ! in a Christian land !
Starved, with wealth on every hand,
Dying outside the pauper's doles,
While pamper'd pride in its thousands rolls.

LORD, HELP THE POOR.

Lord, help Thou the poor,
   Down-trodden and low ;
Lighten their burden
   Of soul-sick'ning woe ;
Scorn'd by the haughty and proud,
   Dry Thou their tears ;
Though wrapp'd in poverty's cloud,
   Soothe Thou their fears ;
   In their distress
   Pity and bless—
     Lord, help the poor.

Thee only they know
   As loving and kind :
So gentle and good,
   Thou'st healed the blind ;
Nor curses nor rude words fall,
   Dear Lord, from Thee :
Blessings Thou givest to all,
   Loving and free :
   Thou art our stay,
   Kneeling we pray—
     Lord, help the poor.

Through darkness and gloom
   Bright sun-gleams shall shine,
Radiant with light
   And glory that's Thine ;
Men may but hate, not so Thou :

Love is thy name ;
Knowing Thee, adoring we bow,
Saviour who came :
Hearing our cry,
Thou'lt not deny—
Lord, help the poor.

OOR AIN WEE BAIRN.*

Bonnie wee totikins,
Bricht as a bee,
Cheeks aye sae rosy red
Brimfu' o' glee.
Mither's sweet petikins,
Faither's wee joy,
Fillin' the hoose wi' bliss,
Free o' alloy.

Darlin' wee lauchin' face,
Een bricht an' blue ;
Kisses like hinny draps
Come frae that mou'.
In a' the warld wide
Nane crouser craw,
Goud canna buy oor bairn,
Bonnie an' braw.

* This, at the request of the Publisher, and the following song,
are inserted in the nursery section of the unique and famous collection
of songs known as " Whistle-Binkie."—pp. 128-134 , vol. ii., edition
1890.

Denty wee dauted bairn,
  Twa spurrin' feet,
Kickin' wi' lifieness
  Chubby hands meet.
A'thing maun pleasure thee,
  King owre us a',
Oh, may nae blightin' blast
  On thy life fa'.

ROBIN A-REE.

Bairnie sae blythe an' fair—
  Robin A-Ree ;
Thy wee heart kens nae care,
  Robin A-Ree ;
Fillin' oor hame wi' joy,
Weavin' sweet spells fu' coy :
Heaven bless thee, my boy—
  Robin A-Ree.

Bricht are thy een sae blue,
  Robin A-Ree ;
Dearly oor bairn we lo'e—
  Robin A-Ree ;
Juist like a fairy neat :
Lips ripe wi' kisses sweet :
Brawer bairn nane can meet—
  Robin A-Ree.

Oor best care ever thine—
    Robin A-Ree ;
Love's spell around thee twine,
    Robin A-Ree ;
Angels, frae scenes sae fair,
Shall bring rich blessin's rare,
To bless thee ever mair—
    Robin A-Ree.

TO THEE I'LL BE TRUE.

One kiss, love, I crave from those beautiful lips,
    One kiss ere I bid thee adieu ;
And though I may wander from thee far away
    My heart, love, shall ever be true—
    To thee it shall ever be true.

One glance, love, I ask from those bright, sparkling eyes,
    Full of love so tender and true ;
For sympathy dwells like a spirit of light
    In the depths of their beautiful blue—
    In their soul-stirring depth of sweet blue.

One clasp, love, I seek of that fair hand of thine,
    While, dearest, my vow I renew,
Till life shall sink down in the stillness of death
    To thee, love, I'll ever be true—
    Yes, changeless to thee I'll be true.

THIS LASSIE O' MINE.

Like the gouden glint o' the simmer sun
    Is the licht o' my lassie's e'e,
An' her lauchter sweet is sae fu' o' fun
    That Love's rich spell she twines roon' me.
An' the bonnie blush on her fair saft cheek
    The brawest rose can ne'er ootshine ;
Though the wide, wide warl' ye may eident seek
    Ye'll no find a lassie like mine.

I've trysted her aft by the siller stream,
    Far doon in the daisy deck'd dell,
An' life seems to me like a fairy dream
    As roon' my heart she twines love's spell.
To my lassie fair I'll ever be true,
    My love for her it winna dwine ;
For a gem my heart can treasure an' lo'e,
    Is this blythesome lassie o' mine.

A SCREED FRAE LIFE.

AN EPISTLE TO J. S., "BON ACCORD."

> We labour soon, we labour late
>   To feed the titled knave, man,
> An' a' the comfort we're to get
>   Is that beyond the grave, man.'

BURNS.

Here dreamin' owre my books I coo'r,
While day dwines fast to gloamin' 'oor
    An' wark wi' me is dune ;
Then ere I ken a weel-faured queen
Comes jinkin' ben wi' witchin' e'en—
    We've woo'd baith late an' sune.
The Muse she's named, an' wi' a smile
    She's gi'en me weft an' warp
To weave a sang in hamely style
    Upon my rough-strung harp.
        Sae here, then, I steer, then,
            To strike the tunefu' string,
        Serenely an' freen'ly
            To you the sang I bring.

What's human griefs ?   Ay, what are they
But torture on life's weary way ?
    If but the heart can feel
The stingin' pains, the sair-wrung sighs
That end wi' deep, despairin' cries
    When reason's made to reel ;

For little " love " is shed abroad
    Where " self " hauds weel her grip,
Though crush'd the heart 'neath poortith's load
    Some ply the maister whip,
        An' sneerin', an' jeerin',
           They tell the waefu' wicht,
        To gain it an' hain it,
           The gear that shines fu' bricht.

Could they but read ilk toiler's heart
Wha eager in life's busy mart
    Haud's thrang frae morn till nicht,
Nor fears to wipe the honest sweat
Frae brows that ne'er were born to fret
    Nor bear the scorner's slicht ;
Hoo strange it is, yet true, I ween,
    The sons o' toil maun slave
For sic a scanty pittance gi'en—
    Scarce ane a groat can save.
        But reivin', deceivin',
           A few the siller gain,
        An' greedy, nor needy,
           They claim it a' their ain.

Wi' upraised hands an' menseless fraise
There's some declare that laws plain ways
    Teach what's ordain'd maun be ;
Sic haivers common sense dings doon,
Though steevly argued by ilk loon
    Wha'd haud the truth ajee ;

Then hate wi' a' its cank'rous train
　　Flows siccar owre the land,
An' conscience pleads for love in vain—
　　Few heed its wise demand.
　　　　But seizin' an' squeezin'
　　　　　The life frae oot the heart,
　　　　They'll argue an' bargue
　　　　　An' play the miser's part.

What's born within it maun come oot
Is true, indeed, nae ane can doot ;
　　But self the planter is
O' sins, the Po'ers abune are blamed
Wi' plantin' there, an' cursed an' shamed
　　Wi' robbin' man o' bliss ;
Ye thochtfu' weel life's pages scan
　　And learn the truth, nor spurn
The fact—'tis man's sad acts to man
　　Gars thoosands heart-sair mourn.
　　　　Then feel it, heart-seal it,
　　　　　Nor fear to let fouk ken
　　　　We're brithers to ithers
　　　　　Wha claim the name o' men.

Losh, you an' me can lift oor e'en
An' view wi' joy ilk wudland scene,
　　Sweet rill, an' bosky dell ;
An' risin' far abune earth's din
Wi' a' its sorrows an' its sin—
　　We scarce daur seek to tell—

The lav'rock's blythsome notes o' sang
    Ring oot sae grand an' clear,
The rich, the puir amang earth's thrang
    The God-gift weel may hear.
        An' cheery, nor weary
           We watch its upward flicht,
        While singin' 'tis wingin'
           Mair near the gates o' licht.

The flo'ers that bloom on ilka brae
An' beautify life's thorny way
    Are gems that cheer the e'e ;
The blushin' rose, the hawthorn tree,
The blue-bell sweet, an' gowans wee,
    Weave spells round you an' me ;
Our roadsides a' are clad wi' flo'ers
    We lo'e but canna name,
They wake fair dreams o' brichter bo'ers
    Where nane ken poortith's shame.
        But flytin' an' bitin',
           The strife o' earth draws near,
        Then weary an' dreary
           Hearts dwine wi' grief an' fear.

Hech ! sic a wecht frae souls 'twad lift
Gin men wad learn that gear's a gift
    To bless their brithers a' ;
Hoo sune wad cease the waefu' sigh,
The sick'nin' moan, starvation's cry
    That thoosands noo let fa',

An' doots an' fears o' God abune
    Sae mony round us hae ;
E'en take my word, they'd vanish sune
    Like nicht before the day.
      Receive it, believe it,
        The truth when plainly tauld ;
      Unfeelin', wha's stealin'
        Life's gear frae young an' auld.

Were heaven gain'd by wealth o' gear
The poor sma' chance wad hae, I fear,
    To tread ilk gowden street ;
But love, to man a gift divine,
Through faith makes heaven yours an' mine—
    There a' may joyous meet.
Then though o' wealth we ne'er hae routh
    While life we battle through,
Let's heart an' soul cling to the truth
    That hames us 'mang the true.
      Where never, forever,
        Sad tears shall dim the e'e,
      Forgiven in heaven
        We'll rest an' thankfu' be.

D

DREAMIN'S O' CHILDHOOD.

Oh, sweet are my dreams o' the days o' my childhood,
   Ere life's trials cam' wi' heart wearin' care ;
'Twas then that I rov'd o'er the hill an' the wildwood,
   Where flow'rs richly bloom'd wi' beauty sae fair.
An' love in my heart for ae lassie was reigning,
   A lassie sae guileless wi' bricht beamin' e'e ;
Oh, Love's spell sae sweet ! we ne'er thocht o' its waning,
   But ever I dreamt that my ain she wad be.
           Oh, childhood's dreams !

An' weel do I mind o' the wee birdies singin'
   Till lood rang the plantin' wi' their blithesome lays,
An' sae sweet to my ears fond mem'ry is bringin'
   The laughter that rang o'er the gowan-clad braes.
The bonnie, braw bairnies had hearts o' the lichtest,
   An' like stars shone life's-licht in ilka clear e'e,
But ever I thocht that lassie the brichtest,
   For love made her fill life's picture wi' me.
           Oh, childhood's dreams !

Oh, the auld carle Time brings changes fu' mony,
   An' lang years hae pass'd sin' l met ane an' a'
O' the dear anes wha play'd 'mang scenes rare an' bonnie,
   In dreams o' sweet fancy ilk ane I reca'.
E'en noo as I gaze on the loch o' The Haining
   An' wander 'mang beauty sae dear unto me
In dreams, like a queen there's ane o'er me reigning,
   A blushin' wee lassie sae fain wad I see.
           Oh, childhood's dreams !

AT THE COWDENKNOWES.

The Simmer's come, an' we maun leave
    The toon wi' a' it's carkin' care,
For toil-worn hearts wad ken the joys
    That lie in Nature's smiles sae rare.
Then wake the charms that gleam fu' grand
    Where Leader streams their beauty bring,
And dreams of fancy draw us on,
    While tender voices thrilling sing—
      "O, the broom, the bonnie, bonnie broom,
      The broom of the Cowdenknowes."
      Wi' lichtsome hearts we'll wanton stray
      Where the broom in beauty grows.

Blythe, blythe the wee birds tune their pipes
    Oot owre the braes and thro' the trees,
But blyther hearts will beat wi' joy
    Where Leader sings upon the breeze.
It comes to view : we dream nae mair,
    Nor lichter hearts e'er beat in kings,
Enchantment lends her richest spells,
    Oor joy-thrill'd heart in gladness sings—
      "O, the broom, the bonnie, bonnie broom,
      The broom of the Cowdenknowes."
      Wi' lichtsome hearts we'll wanton stray
      Where the broom in beauty grows.

Away dull thochts that darken life,
   Sae kindly hope reigns owre it a',
And beauty smiles 'mid pleasure's charms,
   While fairy spells sae richly fa'.
Lang may it bloom, the bonnie broom,
   Wi' a' the flo'ers that roond it spring,
An' lovin' hearts reap Nature's bliss
    Where Leader's waters softly sing—
      " O, the broom, the bonnie, bonnie broom,
        The broom of the Cowdenknowes."
      There lichtsome hearts may wanton stray
        Where the broom in beauty grows.

THE MAIDEN OF TO-DAY.

See that pretty, smiling maiden,
She with dainty fashions laden,
So lightly tripping down the street,
Bewitching all whom she may meet.

Such a natty jockey bonnet,
Not an eye but's fixed upon it ;
And such a fine " improver," too,
Improving nature to the view.

And see that fringe of lovely hair
That's hanging o'er her brow so fair ;
There's a charm that hangs about it,
Only fools will sneer and flout it.

But who can sketch that maiden neat,
Who does so oft parade the street,
When at home ?—not for a pension
What she's there should we e'er mention.

What will she be when she is won,
By silly *dude* who woo'd for fun,
Or some unthinking son of toil
Who's gulled and caught in love's sweet coil ?

Yes, oft that question will arise
As gay she flits before our eyes—
What can those hands have learn'd to do ?
Well may we ask and wonder, too.

She can glide through dances pretty,
Sing a gay and senseless ditty,
And simper smart things, oh, so shy,
With blushing cheeks and downcast eye.

And, with a voice of music mellow,
Talk of " old woman " and " old fellow,"
Sneers and pouts whene'er she names them,
Boasts how for her wants she tames them.

But how to cook, or wash, or sew,
Make no mistake, she does not know ;
Such pretty " toys," it seems to me,
The slattern wife will only be.

'Tis a portrait I have painted—
Are you with this maid acquainted ?
Toss not your head, nor sneer, nor frown,
There's many such within our town.

SONG OF THE MAIDENS OF TO-DAY.

Hurrah ! hurrah ! for the hunting ground,
'Tis there every night we're busy found,
Smiling, laughing, and talking to all,
Angling for husbands short or tall.

Faint not maidens, we shall make men yield
To the siren spell we ever wield ;
For evil talk not a jot care we
If only to us men bow the knee.

By the gutter-side we'll stand of a night,
Tho' with chilling cold our lips grow white ;
There, for a purpose, we laugh or sigh,
Heedless of health or of passers by.

Though bitter tears we yet may shed,
O'er the weary way our lives we've led,
Banish such thoughts and push on the strife,
Till we've gain'd our aim—the name of wife.

Love is a sham, or a story old
That in tale or song is oft-times told,
But 'tis a power that's unknown to-day—
No time have we for such silly play.

Come, maidens, come, let us down the street,
All tripping along so trim and neat ;
Nothing shall daunt us, we're sure to win,
Though deep we may sink ourselves in sin

For what to us is the slur of shame ?
We'll hide it soon 'neath another name ;
Shame ! 'tis found where we eagerly wait,
Looking for him whom we count our fate.

'Tis true our hearts hate life's weary toil,
The better for us our spells soon coil
Around some form, be it dark or fair;
If only a *man*, that's all we care.

Come as he likes, teetotaller or sot,
We're ready to tie the marriage knot
That binds our lives together for life,
To bear the names of husband and wife.

Will we make good wives ? Bother the thought,
They'll have to take us just as they ought,
Unlearn'd, nor ever seeking to learn
Lessons of life and its duties stern.

The present's ours, the future we'll know,
Though the wheels of time grind ever slow ;
We live for the hour that's fleeting by,
As we find our needs we laugh or cry.

Then hurrah, hurrah for the busy street,
Hurrah, hurrah, for the *men* we meet ;
There's glorious sport on our hunting ground,
And like maidens *true* we there are found.

MAIDENS, LIVE AND DARE.

Live, maidens, live
As God would have you do,
Although temptations vast around you may be cast,
Live to be true.

Dare, maidens, dare
To walk midst toil and strife,
With heart that's ever pure, and faith so firm and sure,
A God bless'd life.

Live, maidens, live
In home or in the street,
That satirical sneers, sounding harsh on the ears,
May ne'er thee greet.

Dare, maidens, dare,
To scorn all words impure,
Where'er they may be said, reviling God or maid,
Such ne'er endure.

Live, maidens, live
We need each cheering smile,
As o'er life's flowing tide we ever onward glide
Nor would know guile.

THE HAMELESS BAIRN.

There's bliss in the glint o' the sun's rich beams
When they fa' like goud on the wimplin' streams,
An' a tender cord will wauken'd be
When the birds lilt sae blythe their sangs o' glee,
An' the charm's fu' rare o' the bonnie flo'ers
That we aft-times pu' in the simmer 'oors ;
But litheless an' cauld as the heart o' airn
Is the life that's kent by the hameless bairn.

It makes the heart sair to see the wee form
When fierce blaw the blasts o' the winter's storm,
Sae frichten'd she coo'rs ; she trembles wi' fear
When anger's harsh voice fa's lood on her ear.
The face o' her mither the bairn ne'er saw,
An' better a faither she'd ne'er ha'en ava
Than he wha thus wanders sae reckless an' stern—
Love fills nae the heart o' the hameless bairn.

The blythe birdies ken o' their hames in the dell
When wingin' in flicht owre the muirland fell,
But the bairn dreams nane o' joys she should ken
'Mid the noisesome din o' the wand'rers den.
Oh, pity the bairn, dicht the tear frae her e'e,
An' treat her as weel's your ain bairnies wee :
Kind deeds bring rewards ilk ane weel may learn,
Gin love guides the heart to the hameless bairn.

A DIRGE—JAMES CURRIE.

Born June, 24, 1829.   Died September 5, 1890.

The golden glow of the Autumn sun
   Stream'd rich o'er the laden fields,
And a pensive gladness lit the earth—
   To which the heart responsive yields.
Yet strange—the winds seem'd to whisper soft,
   With a zephyr's gentle breath,
And the woodland singers hushed their songs
   At the minstrel's hour of death.

By the war-worn sword his harp was hung,
   When the vet'ran sank to rest
In the sleep from which none wake on earth,
   Heaven's portal for the blest.
Oh, mystic Death, that stills the heart
   Of the lov'd, the true and brave ;
That dims the eyes with tears of grief
   By the silent new-made grave.

Autumn's rich month, September fair,
   Full clad with harvest glow,
The reapers of earth and the reaper Death
   Make the fruits of earth lie low.
And the mists of grief shroud all around
   As the sting of pain sinks deep,
For the voice we loved has sunk in death
   Like a babe that falls asleep.

And we bow the head and mourn the dead,
    The husband, the father true,
The friend of the widow and orphan child—
    For none ere a kinder knew.
The joy of life seem'd to fade away
    Like flowers of summer time,
Till a voice like a passing sigh came soft—
    " We'll meet in a fairer clime."

Oh, Grave, to thee the crumbling dust we give;
    But back to the God Who gave
By faith the Spirit hath wing'd its flight
    Through the Christ Who died to save;
Where the harp that sang of earth's sweet joy
    Shall wake in the heavenly land,
And sing of the bliss of eternal peace
    Found alone at God's right hand.

STILL TRUST ON.

ADDRESS TO A YOUNG FRIEND.

Welcome, sister, welcome ever are thy smiles of truth and
    love,
In thy fair sweet maiden beauty may thy heart still faith-
    ful prove;
True and tender, wav'ring never, come what will in daily
    strife,
Sink not down despairing-hearted, cling to God the source
    of life.

Shadows oft may cross life's pathway, hiding in their
    shades thy bliss,
Look above thee, faith's revealing there's a brighter sphere
    than this,
There's a land of love and glory, and its dwellers know no
    care :
In the Christ of God still trusting we can sing—" My home
    is there."

From amid the world's sorrows let thy voice ring forth in
    song,
'Tis a gift from God our Father winning souls from sin and
    wrong ;
Song inspirĕd, who can measure all the power that lies in
    thee,
Like a voice from Heaven wafted come those soothing tones
    to me.

Thus have I when weak and weary, faint in heart, and eyes
    grown dim,
Listened 'mid life's ceaseless battle for thy soul-inspiring
    hymn ;
Sweet it rose from heart ne'er dreaming one would catch
    the cheering strain,
And from out the world's turmoil wake to fight its strife
    and pain.

True it is that Christ-like actions stir the soul from woe's
    dark spell,
Till the heart by hope inspirĕd stoops to drink from love's
    sweet well ;

Though the godless, cold and heartless, sneering, jeering,
  dare annoy,
May that one by such undaunted forward press in new-
  born joy.

Not to grief nor tears of sorrow were we born to suffer
  here,
Not to brood o'er sin and cursing till the brain grows mad
  with fear ;
But to live in faith and gladness, led by God's own loving
  hand,
Knowing when we've trod life's pathway we shall reach
  our Fatherland.

Youth is thine, and so light-hearted thou wilt face the
  world's ways,
Dreaming not that evils dreary thou mayst meet in coming
  days ;
Still trust on, nor ever fearing, faith in God o'er death and
  sin,
Though through weakness thou wert dying victor proving
  thou would'st win.

Singing ever, loving sister, let us cheer our fellows on,
Gifts from God are freely given, that His work on earth be
  done ;
Sing and work, though some prove careless, know 'tis what
  on earth we do,
Wins the crown and joyous welcome, " Well done thou who
  hast prov'd true."

Part, ah ! no, we must not sever, joys of Earth and Heaven
     we share,
Through that love which knows no ending, each heart sings
     " My home is there."
Trusting ever, fair sweet sister, let us walk through Earth's
     strange throng,
Till we've passed the golden portals where we'll join the
     Heaven-born song.

A MORNING IN MAY.

The morning sun has kiss'd the hills,
And rich it gleams on tinkling rills ;
The sweet flowers bathed in dews of May
Their beauties to the eye display,
While floating on the sighing breeze,
From uplands fair and budding trees
Comes the rich trill of blackbird's song,
Swift answered by a countless throng—
The linnet, wren, and mellow thrush,
Big with their notes from bank and bush ;
The mavis and the yorling, too,
Their notes the vale ring through and through ;
And see the leader of the choir,
The lark, to Heaven's gates aspire,
As though to catch the notes of song
That ring the golden streets along.

Oft, oft within the scented dell,
Thus Nature's anthems grandly swell ;
While lazy mists but slowly rise,
Disclosing bright the azure skies,
Sweet flow the ever-murm'ring rills
Like silver threads adown the hills,
Where moorfowl sleep by martyrs' graves,
And the bracken wild in grandeur waves.

Thus morn awakes from night's calm sleep
When all rich summer joys may reap,
And those from toil so glad set free,
Would follow with the busy bee
From sweet to sweet, from flower to flower,
Ne'er dreaming of each passing hour,
Enough to feel no weary care,
Enough to wander anywhere ;
Kind Nature how it soothes to rest,
And makes the heart so richly blest.

TO A COMPANION OF CHILDHOOD.

"My dearest meed, a friend's esteem and praise,
To you I sing."

—Burns.

Rich the spell of friendly feeling
    Draws my heart so near to thine ;
Strange sweet charm, the truth revealing
    Thou art led by love divine.
Never once, 'mid years' swift fleeting,
    Joy have I e'er found like this ;
Springing from a gladsome meeting,
    Full of heart-enthralling bliss.

Mem'ry quickly backward glancing,
    Sees again in bygone years
Eyes of beauty brightly dancing,
    Full of joy, or dimm'd with tears.
Hours of childhood ! happy ever !
    Pictured fair on fancy's wings,
Borne away on life's strange river,
    To thy joys my heart still clings.

List, the laughter richly ringing
    Down the years like music sweet ;
From the woodland echoes bringing,
    Making childhood's joys complete.
Can it be that I am dreaming
    As I greet thee once again ?
Dear loved scenes are round us teeming
    Rare in spells that know no wane.

Once again I proudly wander
  'Neath the shadow of the trees,
Drinking deep of Nature's grandeur,
  Feel the kiss of sighing breeze.
Then my bosom glows with pleasure
  As I clasp thy friendly hand ;
Words thy lips let fall I treasure,
  Seeming touched with magic wand.

Who has tasted aught of sadness,
  Drunk the cup of sorrow deep,
Dreamt that there is naught of gladness
  Dropping tears that eyes will weep,
They can know the tender feeling
  Sympathy so sweetly brings—
Through the soul 'tis gently stealing,
  As if borne on angel wings.

Free from all the pride and scorning,
  Vain weak hearts within them grow,
Thou art well thy sphere adorning,
  Joys around thee richly flow.
True the promise ever proving,
  Given in sweet childhood's days,
That thy heart is kind and loving,
  Trammelled not with world's ways.

Life is oftimes fraught with sorrow,
  Fainting hearts grow weak with care ;
How they long some brighter morrow
  May bring of joys a fuller share :

E

But each one feels life's way brightened
    By such cheering words as thine ;
Thus the weary soul is lightened
    With the light of love divine.

Ne'er may clouds of darkening sorrow
    Dim the lustre of thine eye ;
May the joys of each good morrow
    Prove foretastes of bliss on high.
When the night comes slowly creeping
    Down the hills and o'er the lea,
May One guard thee gently sleeping,
    Rarest friend of all to me.

THE AULD FOLK.

Oh, the auld folk, the auld folk,
    Are wearin' doon the brae ;
Their steps are gettin' slower noo,
    Their heids are unco grey.
Fu' weel they've warsled through the past
    Mid trials they hae ha'en,
An' sair we'll miss the dear auld folk
    When frae us they are ta'en.

Oh, the auld folk, the auld folk,
    Wi' muckle furthy glee
Hae seen around their cosie hearth
    Their ain bairns' bairnies wee.

They've heard them sabbin' sair wi' grief,
   They've seen them blithe and gay,
An' aye their hearts lap hie wi' joy
   To hear the bairns at play.

Oh, the auld folk, the auld folk,
   Wi' hearts sae warm an' true,
While we are wi' them here oorsel's
   We winna cease to lo'e.
We'll dae oor best to cheer them aye
   While trudgin' owre life's road—
Wi' kindly words an' lovin' smiles
   We'll mak' them feel fu' snod.

Oh, the auld folk, the auld folk,
   When they are laid at rest
Within the grave, we'll plant braw flow'rs
   Abune ilk dear lo'ed breast.
An' far abune yon bricht blue sky,
   In heavenly mansions fair,
We'll meet the couthie guid auld folk—
   We'll meet to pairt nae mair.

BY YON LOCH SIDE.

I love to roam at e'en
    By yon loch side,
Where blossom haw an' gean
    By yon loch side
Sae matchless an' sae fair ;
There's beauty dwelling there.
I'd bide for evermair
    By yon loch side.

There's flo'ers o' ilka hue
    By yon loch side,
Ilk bonnie ane we lo'e
    By yon loch side ;
Fu' saftly blaws the breeze
Wi' music mang the trees
The heart wi' bliss to heeze,
    By yon loch side.

'Tis like some fairy scene
    By yon loch side,
Bewitchin' heart an' een
    By yon loch side ;
In sunshine or in snaw
Some spell the heart can draw
Frae weary strife awa'
    By yon loch side.

The mavis sweetly sings
   By yon loch side,
Till hill an' woodland rings
   By yon loch side ;
An' fancy on her wing
The vanish'd days aft bring,
When bairnies we wad sing
   By yon loch side.

BONNIE, BLYTHESOME MAY.

Oh, bonnie, blythesome May we ne'er can forget
The days o' langsyne—oor frolics we mind yet ;
For sweet were bairnhood's joys, but, 'tween you an' me,
In the years to come their like we ne'er shall see.

Nae care had we then —wi' the birds we wad sing,
Or thrang wi' oor games we danced in a ring ;
An' like a fairy queen—ye mind hoo sae slee—
Wi' nae words ye'd tease but the glance o' your e'e.

We wander'd in simmer the braw flo'ers to pu'—
Though some spak o' ithers my heart warm'd to you ;
Wi' cheeks like the roses an' een fu' o' glee,
Oh, bonnie, sweet May, there was nae ane like thee !

Ye ken in a' the toon nane fairer we saw,
An' like subjects true, your look or word was law ;
It needna be wonder'd that witch'ry sae slee
Young hearts would steal e'er they kent what love could be.

But a' had to pairt—ilk ane their gate has gane ;
Some lie in the kirkyard, some sail'd owre the main ;
But bonnie, blythesome May, forgot ye ne'er shall be,
An' the dear langsyne when we were bairnies wee.

AULD SCOTLAND'S HEATHER BELLS.

Gae bring me frae the green hillsides,
    Auld Scotland's heather bells,
Gae pu' them when the lav'rock's sang
    In richest grandeur swells.
For weel I lo'e the bonnie flow'rs
    That deck oor mountain land,
There canna be ayont the sea
    A flo'er that's hauf sae grand.

        Dear heather bells, sweet heather bells,
           In gentle lady's bow'r,
        Though rich and rare, though bright and fair,
           Like thee there's no a flow'r.

Its fragrance mingled wi' ilk breeze
    When Wallace led the brave ;
When Forth's clear tide was crimson dyed,
    And foemen found a grave ;
And nobler seem'd its purple hues
    When Bruce at Bannockburn
Made Tyrant's chain sink wi' the slain
    In death, ne'er to return.

        Dear heather bells, &c.

Then frae oor ain hillsides gae bring
    The weel lo'ed heather bells,
Gae pu' them where the bracken waves
    On a' oor muirs and fells.
For I would weave a glorious wreath
    To crown yon lassie's broo,
Whose sweet voice rings while weel she sings
    Your praise, dear flow'r we lo'e.
        Dear heather bells, &c.

MOTHER.

What is this bright angels whisper
    In a sweet heart-thrilling tone ?
Golden harps in music breathe it
    By the great eternal throne.
'Tis a word on earth the sweetest
    Ever lisp'd by mortal tongue,
Like a gem in song entrancing
    Round the heart its charms are flung ;
Bless'd by Him who gave it being,
    'Tis a word that speaks of love ;
Bend and list, oh list to catch it,
    Zephyrs bear it from above.
        Peerless name o'er father, brother,
        Is the dear lov'd one of Mother.

Robed in royal purple splendour,
   Jewel-crown'd in palace great,
Child of toil in humble vestments
   Sorrow's burden oft thy fate ;
Deep in wealth's intense elation,
   Misery crouching in the street,
Murmur with a tender accent
   That one word in love so sweet.
Hearts sin-stain'd from madness turning,
   Breathe it with love's soften'd sigh,
And the meek One in compassion
   Spake it ere He bow'd to die.
     Peerless name o'er every other
     Is the dear lov'd one of Mother.

THE HONEST AN' LEAL.

Ye wild winds blaw saft roond the hames o' the leal,
Oor heart's wish is this—may they ever be weel,
May health kiss their cheeks an' guid meat fill their store,
While sorrow gangs swiftly awa' frae their door.
Wi' love on them beamin', the blythesome and leal,
Their cup wi' bliss reamin' fu' thankfu' will feel,
That hearts sinkin' weary through trials sae dreary,
They help to make cheerie up life's brae to speel.

Hoo hearty the laugh o' the honest an' leal,
Sae fearless their words they gar Tyranny reel,
The grasp o' their hands makes the heart beat fu' warm,
Their friendship has ever a life-givin' charm,
The dowie soul thrillin'.   Though dark cluds o' wae
Ilk breast wad be fillin', through life's tangled day
Sae hearty they're singin' love's anthem lood ringin',
Till, hope brichter springin', we'll fearna life's fray.

Then hail to the hearts that are honest an' leal,
An' bricht lowe their hearths is oor wish when we kneel.
Auld Scotland has need o' the manfu' an' true,
Wha'll never let Truth to fause cowardice boo ;
'Mang hatred fu' bitter may gude them defen'.
There's nane can prove fitter than some that we ken
To make the sad cheerie wha're sair worn an' weary
On life's road made dreary through fause-hearted men.

THE BAIRNS.

AIR—" Lang, Langsyne."

Losh ! cauld winter's come again,
An' the snaw cleeds hill an' plain,
An' Jock Frost wi' little fear
Nips the taes an' fingers queer,
While the bairnies big and wee
A' are sclyin' wi' sic glee
  Frae the dawn o' the day till the gloamin'.

There's our Jock an' little Teen,
Fun an' laughter fill their een ;
An' there's Tam, the sturdy loon,
Scarce his like in a' the toon ;
An' there's Rab and Sandy's sel',
Hoo they snawba' a' pell-mell
　　Frae the dawn o' the day till the gloamin'.

An' oh ! sic an awfu' fricht
As we gat the ither nicht
When " Galashens " they would act ;
Our Jock's croon was sairly crack'd,
An' the bluid cam' rinnin' doon—
'Twas the speak o' a' the toon
　　Frae the dawn o' the day till the gloamin'

When their mither brings them in
Hoo they fill the hoose wi' din,
There's sic strampin' wi' their feet,
While some start to fecht an' greet ;
Ithers shoutin' " gie's a piece "—
Losh, her wark it canna cease
　　Frae the dawn o' the day till its gloamin'.

Whiles they're at the curlin' puil
Playin' truant frae the schule,
But at nicht when cuddled doon
Then we straik ilk bonnie croon,
An' we saftly breathe a pray'r
That they'll be oor Faither's care
　　Frae the dawn o' this life till its gloamin'

WOOIN' O' A LASS AT E'EN.

Merrily in the ha' at e'en
    Piper play your chanter,
Ye dinna ken where we hae been
    Ridin' at a canter.
Its goud that wins a lassie's love,
Gude faith she winna fickle prove,
Gin ye hae lands where she may rove,
    Naething then will daunt her.
      Wooin' o' a lass at e'en,
      Wooin' o' a lass at e'en,
      Dinna fear though ye be seen,
      Wooin' o' a lass at e'en.

Sae sleely she will greet your smile,
    Lauchin' fu' o' banter,
Or coyly wi' ilk pawkie wile
    She'll haud by her wanter.
Losh, wooin's quirkie, strange, an' queer,
To win the " Yes " there's whiles a steer,
But haud ye till't an' hae nae fear,
    A' she asks juist grant her.

Lads wha hae toom poortith's purse,
    Dinna gang a wanter,
Nae feelin's fine for you she'll nurse,
    Turn aboot an' canter,
Disdainfu' she will look fu' hie,
A deidly scorn in ilka e'e,
A lad o' siller her's maun be
    Wha will win this daunter

ROBERT BURNS.

And Burns—though brief the race he ran,
  Though rough and dark the path he trod,
Lived—died—in form and soul a man,
  The image of his God.

Fitz-Greene Halleck.

With pride the heart of Scotland owns
  The power of one undying name,
And tens of thousands o'er the earth
    Respond with loud acclaim
The praise of him who sang as ne'er
  Hath sung the voice of poet yet.
Who call their birthland "Scotland dear,"
    Burns' name will ne'er forget.

'Twas not in ivied castle tower
  Where wealth or titled lordlings dwell,
First woke to life, that song-wrapt soul
    Who threw o'er all a spell ;
The lowly cot, the peasant's home,
  Where worth rejoiced in love-won bliss,
When winter blew her wildest blasts,
    There dawn'd that life of his.

" Cauld Januar win's " how like were ye
  To cold neglect that babe would know,
Ere 'mid the changing scenes of time
            He'd leave all earth-born woe !
And yet that infant held a gift
  Within his soul mankind would praise,
And crown old Scotland's mountain land
            With wealth of deathless lays.

The harvest field with golden grain,
  The Nith's and Doon's fair winding streams,
The mountain daisy, " crimson-tipp'd,"
            Became to him sweet themes ;
And who with hearts to freedom bound,
  While rich the life-blood warms their veins,
Can list unmov'd to " Auld Langsyne "—
            Best of lov'd friendship's strains ?

When peal the slogans of our clans,
  And flash the claymores red with gore,
Inspired with " Scots wha hae " they fight
            For Scotland's heath-clad shore ;
And mem'ry dreams of bygone scenes,
  When 'neath some milk-white scented thorn
They pledged their troth to modest worth
            That doth our land adorn.

How oft he touched his harp with skill,
  And sang the praise of maidens fair,
Whose witching glances thrill'd his heart
            By Lugar's stream or Ayr !

Or satirising cant and wrong
  With God-sent power and fire,
Forth flashed the words of truth and right
          From his true Scottish lyre.

Sour-faced " Hypocrisy " then felt,
  With " Superstition " dark and drear,
The swift-wing'd arrows of his gift,
          And, trembling, shook with fear ;
While " Virtue's " praised in manly tones,
  With honest, true, and tender love,
" As rapture, bliss beyond compare,"
          God-given from above.

He had his faults ; what human soul
  E'er lived on earth and knew not sin,
Nor felt the deep, the strange unrest
          That leads to wrong within ?
His faults forgive, and love the good—
  Be that our heart's chief aim through life,
And cheer'd by song's enthralling power
          We 'll lose the sting of strife.

Go learn from him the worth of sense,
  Nor e'er its noble teachings spurn,
Or thou mayst make, as fool have done,
          Our brother man to mourn.
Be led by truth, God-given truth,
  And haste the time from shore to shore,
When man shall claim as brother man
          Each race the world o'er.

Immortal bard ; who thrilling sang
　Those matchless songs that firmer twine
Around our hearts as years roll by,
　　　Bright growing fame is thine.
And though poor carping souls may sneer,
　Their scorn or hate the true Scot spurns,
And fearless tells we love our bard
　　　The brave soul'd Robert Burns

BIRTHDAY MUSINGS.

We view, as in a dream, the years swift gone,
And wonder if they've pass'd us one by one,
   A child at play, a boy at school when dreams
   Arose, bright as the sheen of sun-kiss'd streams.

In youth, sweet fancy revel'd in the years
Hid in futurity, nor had we fears
   Sad pain, not joy, might tread with us life's road.
Ah ! life how strange art thou ; hid from our eyes
Unseen behind Time's veil the future lies ;
   But moments come to make or mar for God.

In manhood we can see mistakes now past,
   And shun temptations luring baneful pow'r ;
   So living, that in each swift passing hour
We know on whom our every care is cast.

A SANG TO MYSEL'.
AIR—"Rothesay Bay"—adapted.

Hoo some jeer me in the mornin',
   Ay, an' a' the lee-lang day,
Sin' I winna keep frae rhymin',
   While I climb life's crookit brae.
Losh, it keeps me blythe an' heartsome,
   An' the teardraps frae ilk e'e—
'Tis a gift frae Ane abune us ;
   Sae they needna fash wi' me.

True, their words sometimes cut keenly,
    As their tongues wag croose an' free ;
But I'll heedna, though I'm slichted ;
    Silly fules whiles tak' the gee.
Be they freend or frem'd wha meddle,
    In the morn or gloamin' grey,
I'll e'en wake the harp that's gi'en me,
    An' I'll sing my simple lay.

Na, I canna tell folk's meanin',
    Hoo they rin the sang gift doon ;
For they'll sit an' fret an' yaumer
    'Neath a black an dreary froon.
But e'en be it dule or sunshine,
    They come a' the same to me,
Sin' I lo'e the Ane abune us,
    An' His gift that's gi'en me glee.

THE LASSIE WHA'S A'THING TO ME.

The sun's dwinin' doon, an' 'twill sune be awa'—
The silence o' gloamin' aroond us will fa' ;
Wi' heart beatin' true 'neath the auld trystin' tree,
I'll meet wi' the lassie wha's a'thing to me.

The lav'rock's at rest frae his flicht up abune,
The blackbird is noo wi' his pairtin' saug dune,
The flow'rs are a' closed on the hill an' the lea,
I'll meet wi' the lassie wha's a'thing to me.

There's something aboot her I canna weel tell,
A something that thraws roond my heart a sweet spell.
Oh, where lies its po'er, in her voice or her e'e ?
I'll ken when I meet her wha's a'thing to me.

She charms na' wi' goud wha has nae goud ava',
But her voice on my ear like music will fa'—
The sweet, modest blush, while her sweet lips I pree,
Gars me lo'e weel the lass wha's a'thing to me.

Sweet laughter rings licht frae her lips on the air—
It fa's like a balm on the heart that is sair ;
She feels for the sad, an' kind words she can gie,
Can the bonny blythe lass wha's a'thing to me.

I weel lo'e the tryste-hour that sune will be here ;
An' tenderly then there's ae question I'll spier—
Gin she'll name the day when we twa ane shall be—
Sae dear is that lassie wha's a'thing to me.

THE WINTER'S WEARY CRY.

They have felt it, oh, my brothers—
  They have felt the want of bread :
Mothers weeping in starvation,
  Children drifting to the dead,
Whilst the tempests wildly raging
  Fill the home with sadness drear,
Till the heart with sorrow burdened
  Sinks to earth in bitter fear.

Oh, my brothers, God in heaven
  Never sent the sick'ning gloom
That makes souls, of life grown weary,
  Long for rest within the tomb.
Whom, then, shall we blame for aiding
  All this sorrow and heart pain ?
And the wild winds seem to answer—
  ' Ask ye not a question vain ? '

Is it vain to ask it, brothers,
  'Mid their tears and heart-wrung sighs,
Whilst around us starving wretches
  For the life-bread raise their cries,
And around us there are many
  Who scarce feel the winter's cold ?
Who are cloth'd and fed in plenty,
  Pampered with their wealth of gold.

Oh, the wan and weary children,
  Is it well that they should weep,
Or that 'mid the night hours dreary
  Mothers wake and cannot sleep,

Whilst the haunting dreams oppress them
   Of starvation dank and bare,
And breaks the dawn as daylight cometh,
   Weighted with its cross of care?

Fathers, in the strength of manhood,
   Fain would seek to win through toil
Fruits from out the world's commerce,
   Fruits from out the yielding soil.
Yes, they toil till growing weakness
   Bids them fall amid the strife,
And the light of summer gladness
   Fades for ever from their life.

Blame the miser lords of labour—
   They who grasping seize and keep
That which buys the life-bread, brothers,
   That for which the children weep.
Would they knew the home-life dreary
   Lived beside the fireless hearth,
When the seasons' silent changing
   Bid the Frost King bind the earth.

Shall the weeping of the children
   Cease in summer's golden hours,
When the lark is skywards hymning
   O'er the earth rich clad with flowers?
It would surely cease, my brothers,
   'Neath love's sweet and gentle smile;
It shall cease when all hold equal
   Fruits that spring from honest toil.

A PASSIN' THOCHT.

When a' the warld fa's asleep
   An' wakes ayont swift Time—
The blythesome bairn, the lyart pow,
   An' manhood in its prime—

I wonder gin we'll meet, an' be
   Mair kindly than we've been,
Nor waefu' care gar saut, saut tears
   Come drappin' frae the een.

Or will that "something" in the breast
   Still crave for something mair,
E'en be it gowd, the miser's god,
   Or love sae pure an' rare.

True, life an' sleep are unco strange,
   Yet stranger death than a':
Ae lang-drawn breath an' then—ah, me!
   The earth life's passed awa'.

In Faith an' Hope let's gang to sleep,
   Content that death reveals
Enough to make the Spirit blest
   Where never grind Time's wheels.

A SANG O' MEMORY.

AIR—"There's nae luck aboot the hoose."

———

My heart loe's weel that blissfu' time,
  Life's mornin' bein an' braw,
When a' the Peel Gate's blythesome bairns
  In joyous games wad craw.
'Twas music to ilk mither's ear,
  Mair sweet than birds can sing,
When hand in hand we lilted roond
  The merry "jingo-ring."
    Oh, turn the wheels o' Time again,
      Bring back the days sae sweet,
    When care ne'er lined the bonnie broo
      Nor clogg'd the lichtsome feet.

On mem'ry's wings ilk form comes fair,
  I see them ane an' a'—
The witchin' smile, the pawkie wile,
  Their charms wad roond us draw.
Wi' "Yin-ery, Twae-ery" we wad coont
  Wha in oor games were oot ;
At "hide an' seek" sae fu' o' glee
  We chased the 'oors aboot.

Like ither bairns, we whiles cuist oot
  Owre some bit slee-gaun trick,
Or waggish tongues would sair torment
  Till used we neive or stick ;

But bickers sune wad cease atweel,
  Wi' "'Gree, ma bairnies, 'gree,"
An' een wad glint like stars abune
  In glamour wi' oor glee.

The auld toon-heid, 'tis changed indeed ;
  It's no the same ava—
Nae daffin', laughin' bairns are seen,
  Like in the years awa'.
Auld Time has touch'd us wi' his wand,
  An' care sits on ilk broo,
Yet still we treasure like rare gems
  The years o' bairnhood true.

EPISTLE TO ONE ESTEEMED.

"A friend in need 's a friend indeed,'
  So says the old adage and true ;
And in our hours of greatest need
  We found a noble friend in you.
How poor the heart that could refuse
  To touch the harp that would express
A simple tribute of the muse,
  Of Doric rhymes in lowly dress.

Ance mair my harp exultant swells,
Ance mair ilk wild note proodly tells,
  I lo'e dear land but thee !
There may be lands wi' brichter skies,
Where winter storms but seldom rise,
  Yet fairest thou'rt to me.

The grand sangs o' the siller rills,
    Enchanting is their sound,
The beauty o' oor auld grey hills
    Wi' purple heather crown'd
      Still cheer me, endear me
        To a' that's guid an' grand ;
      An' cheerie nor weary
        I'll sing my native land.

Ilk breeze that sweeps alang the braes
Bears on its wings the wild birds' lays,
    Sae soothin' to ilk breast ;
On haugh, an' dell, an' fernieknowe,
Fair flo'er, an' bush, an' rare tree grow
    In beauty o' the best ;
An' grand emotions rise within
    That struggle to be free,
Till shout we 'bune the warld's din,
    "The land o' liberty !"
      Sae queenly, serenely,
        She rides the briny wave,
      An' claims still the name still,
        The free hame o' the brave.

We bauldly boast we'll ne'er be slaves,
For Freedom's flag abune us waves
    Sae glorious an' sae grand ;
The claymore's flashin' in the licht
Restrains the tyrant's hated micht
    Wha'd fain oppress oor land.

But haud awee, there's some we ken
 Forget themsel's fu' sair,
An' trample on their fellow-men,
 Till bosoms heave wi' care.
  An' sighin' an' cryin'
   To Him Wha reigns on hie,
  They ask yet to bask yet
   Where a' frae dule are free.

But cuifs are they wha wad oppress
An' sink their fellows in distress,
 Nor gi'e them leave to toil ;
Nae wonder frae their lips there fa
Dark words averse to Heaven's law,
 An' sin their hearts will coil
Wi' gallin' po'er, till life itsel'
 Seems stamp'd wi' endless pain ;
Nae bliss within their breasts can dwell,
 But, like a very Cain,
  They curse still an' nurse still
   Their hate for ane an' a',
  An' jeerin' an' sneerin'
   They deeper doonward fa'.

'Tis true the warld's cursed wi' shame,
Sae dark, sae wild, we scarce daur name,
 But bauld sic deeds condemn,
An' pleadin' cry, Oh ! brithers, rise !
Wi' pure true hearts, an' kind an' wise,
 The tide o' wrang to stem.

We're no sent here life to destroy,
  Nor cloud it sair wi' sin ;
But that we may drink deep o' joy,
  An' bliss eternal win.
      Sae rise then an' prize then
        The pureness o' the heart,
      Like true men nor rue men
        To act a Christ-like part.

Dear Scotland, land we lo'e sae weel,
In thee we ken there's some wha feel
  For brethren in distress,
Wi' kindly hand they thochtfu' gi'e
What weel they ken will usefu' be,
  Nor ostentatious press
Their gifts before the gaze o' a',
  But silently they've gi'en ;
An' God alane the blessin's saw
  Whilk brocht tears to the een.
      An' prood then they stood then,
        Wha gat but couldna speak ;
      An' prayin' they're sayin'
        Wi' hearts sae low an' meek—

Oh, Thou Wha reign'st owre ane an' a',
An' kindness mak's thy greatest law,
  Bless Thou forever mair
The noble hearts wha thus hae bless'd
The needfu' anes wi' poortith press'd,
  An' eased their hames o' care ;

Be Thou their Guide, be Thou their Stay
    'Mid a' the ills in life ;
May flo'ers bestrew their life's pathway
    Unscaith'd wi' dule or strife.
      " Thou Being all-seeing,
        Hear this oor earnest prayer ;
      Oh, take them and make them
      Thine everlasting care."

Sic frien's we've kent, an' thus we sing
The feelin's that within us spring,
    Though feeble we express
In rustic rhymes the joy o' heart,
The kindly deeds that made them start,
    Yet still we feel nae less.
We're bless'd, an' sae's oor native land,
    That she sic bairns can claim ;
Oh, lang may siclike foremost stand
    An honour to her name.
      Excuse, then, the muse, then,
        That winna silent be ;
      But ringin', 'tis singin'
      These heart-felt rhymes to thee.

COME LET US A' BE CHEERIE.

INSCRIBED TO FOUR POETIC FRIENDS.

Come gather, bardies, ane and a',
Wi' richt guid will attend the ca',
In union sweet fu' crousely craw :
       Come let us a' be cheerie.

     Strike your harps wi' micht and main,
     Drive awa' dull care and pain,
     Gar the roof-tree ring again
       Wi' sangs fu' blythe and cheerie.

Come leave the mill wi' noisy wheels,
Their fearfu' din the heart aft feels,
The sweets o' life frae ilk ane steals—
       Come let us a' be cheerie.

The tangled web juist leave alane,
'Twill a' be richtly placed again
When ye hae sung a blythesome strain—
       Come let us a' be cheerie.

Come spin poetic thochts this nicht,
Gie carkin' care an unco fricht,
Leave pirns and spools for fancy's flicht—
       Come let us a' be cheerie.

Nae langer muse o'er midnicht dreams,
But wake your harp wi' lichter themes :
Shed o'er us a' joy's blissfu' beams—
       Come let us a' be cheerie.

Come gather roond oor sister fair—
Her soul wi' music's filled fu' rare ;
While wi' you a' I'll feel nae care—
  Come let us a' be cheérie.

IN MEMORIAM—THOMAS RAE ("DINO.")

BORN OCT. 19TH, 1868. DIED SEPT. 11TH, 1889.

At rest, lov'd Friend, "beyond all mortal throes,"
No more thou'lt feel earth's weary heart-sick woes ;
 Thou'st reach'd the rest thy soul so long'd to know,
 Past "doubt's dark night" to that rich afterglow,
Which springs from peace and perfect calm through love
Eternal as the sinless land above.

The God who gave thee power midst pain to sing,
 Hath call'd thee, and thou'st hasten'd to obey ;
Untrammell'd thou'lt awake thy harp's new string,
 To songs of bliss through Heaven's eternal day.

'Tis true that grief is ours, though gain is thine,
 When call'd to greet thy smile on earth no more ;
But sweet the thought, the joy shall yet be mine,
 We'll meet and sing where partings are all o'er.

EPISTLE TO WILLIAM WALLACE.

AUTHOR OF "POEMS AND SONGS."

DEAR SIR,
           Though cranky critics cry
  Fu' pithless is my writin',
Will I sae bairnlike girn an' greet,
  Or start sarcastic flytin'?
Haith, sirce, a silly fule I'd be,
  For, freen', believe my wordy,
That aft I rhyme to fleg dull care,
  An' mak' my heart feel sturdy.

Though maybe whiles across my mind
  Some thochts come sleely jinkin',
That I to ithers yet may bring
  Some pleasure wi' my clinkin'.
For weel I ken that sangs ha'e po'er
  To clear the heart o' sorrow,
An' chase the cluds that hide frae view
  The bricht hopes o' the morrow.

Owre aft amid the toils o' life,
  Aroond oor hearts there's twinin'
Some cauldrife spell that gars oor sauls
  In dark despair gae dwinin'.
Sae kennin' this I deem it richt
  To use the gifts God's given
To lift ilk heart aboon dull care,
  An' draw it nearer Heaven.

The wrang I hate, the richt I lo'e,
   Though ithers may keep winkin',
While life is mine I'll fearless strike
   Against a' sin an' drinkin'.
For, oh ! what bliss an' joyousness
   The feck o' folk are losin',
Wha worship self, and daily sink
   Their ain respect in boosin'.

But losh ! I'm wand'rin' far afield,
   An' orra thochts I'm screedin',
Instead o' sayin' that your buik
   Wi' pleasure I've been readin'.
See there's my hand, ye're welcome till't,
   My gifted poet brither,
An' gie me thine, my spirit langs
   That we may meet ilk ither.

" The Burnie " I hae watched like you,
   When blythesome an' sae cheery,
It laughin' sang the fields amang,
   An' blessed the heart fu' weary.
An' oh ! the hills, the " risin' hichts,"
   Where freedom's flag's aye wavin'.
For love o' them wha wadna fecht,
   The micht o' faemen bravin'.

An' upwards " frae the gladd'ning earth "
   I've seen " The Skylark " steerin',
To hymn his thanks at Heaven's gates,
   Near oot o' sicht an' hearin'.

An' hoo my heart danced licht an' free
  As by a hill-path narrow,
In pilgrim mood I wand'rin' gaed
  To far-famed classic " Yarrow."

'Twas glorious on the green hillside
  To gaze, where siller gleamin',
The lo'ed stream ran an' eerie sang,
  An' then to fa' a-dreamin'.
I heard the slogan-cry, an' saw
  Baith sword an' halberd glancin'.
While deep'nin' was the deidly strife,
  An' war steeds wild were prancin'.

Losh, sirce, your muse an' I seem freens,
  " Heart longings " hae been mine, sir,
In " Dreamland " I hae wander'd aft,
  Where fairy ferlies shine, sir.
Through " Buckholm Woods," by Gala's stream,
  At witchin' hours o' gloamin,
When shone the siller-glintin' mune
  I've aftimes gane a-roamin'.

But ilka sang-verse in your buik
  Has set my heart-strings ringin',
An' frae the present an' the past
  Sweet thochts to me is bringin'.
Oh ! Wallace wight, may ye be spared
  Lang years to wake your lyre,
An' cheer the hearts o' ane an' a'
  Wi' true poetic fire.

Nor fear to sing, the joys ye ken
　　Than goud's a greater treasure,
Though siller is fu' guid to hae,
　　It brings nae hauf the pleasure.
I've tasted it when, deep in wae,
　　My heid wi' pain was hinging',
Frae a' sic scaith Guid keep ye free,
　　An' joyous be your singin'.

IN MEMORIAM—WILLIAM WALLACE.

AUTHOR OF " POEMS AND SONGS."

(Born August 6th, 1862 ; died June 20th, 1889.)

He sleeps—the gentle, tired heart's at rest ;
　　His harp is hush'd, unstrung the sweet-ton'd strings
He lov'd so well, and now among the blest
　　He'll live to praise the mighty King of Kings.
Nor city streets shall e'er resound his tread,
　　Nor Border hills, nor banks of flow'r-clad stream,
　　Where, wandering forth, he'd dream some fairy dream,
As fancy oft his wayward footsteps led.
　　At rest, thou gentle, loving song of song !
　　Yes, quit of all the care thou'st known so long.
So young in years we mourn thy going.　Yet,
Thy work 'tis done, then why should we e'er fret ?
　　God's will be ours.　And may thy songs, thy life,
　　Still cheer and strengthen toilers 'mid the strife.

G

A PICTURE FROM LIFE.

" Fools are my theme, let satire be my song."

BYRON.

———

As tread we life's eventful way
Strange beings meet we day by day,
As wide asunder as the poles
Are noble actions from such souls.

Gaze on them as they pass you by,
Low sneaking worms of earth so sly ;
They seem to friendship true—but mark !
They're mask'd to stab you in the dark.

They cringe and fawn with manner meek,
Love seems in every word they speak,
As though had they rich wealth of gold
To aid your needs 'twould down be told.

Religion as a cloak they don
Though in their souls its pow'r's unknown,
No Christ-like deeds reveal a mind
That works through love for human-kind.

As hypocritic crawling worms
Cloth'd in the garb of human forms,
They creep amidst the weak and strong,
And do their cruel deeds of wrong.

In poison dipp'd they drop their words
That gall the breast like rough-edged swords,
Or like a thousand reptile stings
That torture ere release death brings.

See, see how **Judas-like they'll kiss**
Their victims who have lived in **bliss,**
Pure as the purest gem of love
That e'er adorn'd the realms above.

Then watch how in that stream of hate
Their victims meet a sick'ning fate,
Jeer'd by a thoughtless, cruel throng,
They sink, they perish 'neath deep wrong.

See how they blandly bow and smile
Though in their souls they plot the while,
How innocence shall feel their pow'r
And fall in some unguarded hour.

Nor love nor pity ere finds rest
Within a cold and sensual breast,
Such but exist for self alone,
Nor higher Power will they e'er own.

Sleek in the seeming garb of love
So sympathetic on they move
Till Death, dread foe, shall claim his prey,
And thus from earth they pass away.

Ah ! who will mourn them when they're gone ?
The ready answer meets us—None :
For as they've lived so shall they die,
Unhonour'd with a tear or sigh.

THE THISTLE DINGS THEM A'.

(" *Nemo me impune lacessit.*")

AIR—" Scotland Yet."

Gae sing o' England's red, red rose
   In a' its beauty braw,
Or praise the shamrock—Erin's pride—
   Ae flo'er can ding them a'.
Let battles wage or tempests rage,
   In grandeur sae serene,
To yon bricht skies bauld thistles rise
   On Scotia's mountains green ;
For freedom aye 'twill stand or fa'—
   The thistle dings them a'.

Upon the mountain's heath-clad sides,
   Alang the wooded fells,
And through the glens where siller streams
   Entwine the heart wi' spells,
There like a king in regal micht
   The patriot soul to thrill ;
In a' its pride whate'er betide,
   The thistle's blooming still ;
For freedom aye 'twill stand or fa'—
   The thistle dings them a'.

In days o' auld when foemen socht
   The free-born to enslave,
Then leapt the claymore frae its sheath,
   And fearless focht the brave,

And weel the bearded thistle's proved
   It's po'er to aid the cause,
O' freedom's richt and freedom's micht,
   By Nature's glorious laws ;
For freedom aye 'twill stand or fa'—
   The thistle dings them a'.

IN ONE FOND KISS.

Oh, who would seek to break the spell
   That holds the heart in thrall ?
Or yet would seek to mar the joy
   That answers love's sweet call ?
Full rich and tender is its charm,
   Nor life holds sweeter bliss
When heart meets heart and lip meets lip
   In one fond ling'ring kiss.

The wandering zephyrs softly press
   The flowers in beauty rare,
And restless bees on beating wings
   Their honied richness share ;
But thrills the heart with ecstasy,
   The cause 'tis only this,
That love-enchain'd lip meets with lip
   In one fond ling'ring kiss.

At dewy eve love whispers low
  With gentle, trusting smile,
And thrills the oft-times weary heart
  Made faint with grief or toil,
At morn and eve 'tis joy to know
  That each would sadly miss
Love's dear embrace when lip meets lip
  In one fond ling'ring kiss.

OOR AIN LEDDY MAY.

Sic a tot is mither's bairn,
  Fu' o' fun an' glee,
Sic a denty bonnie mou'
  Has oor lassie wee.
Kisses sweet as e'er were gien
  Get we ilka day,
Treasure 'bune a' warl's gear,
  Oor ain Leddy May.

Restless as the waukrife winds,
  Scarce a minute still,
Wantin' a' her een can see,
  Strampin' wi' a will.
Queen owre a' aboot the hoose,
  Nane daur say her nay,
Sic a bairn was never seen,
  Oor ain Leddy May.

Bring a posie o' sweet flo'ers
  Frae the wudlands braw,
She's the fairest flo'er I ken,
  Sweeter than them a'.
Bring her gems frae 'yont the sea,
  Heedna what ye pay,
They're needed a' to please oor bairn,
  Oor ain Leddy May.

Guidness-sakes what ails her noo ?
  Sleepin' like a tap !
Weel-a-weel I'm thankfu' for't,
  I'm maist like to drap.
Yet there's music in her voice,
  Folk can hae their say,
She's a gift frae lands abune
  Oor ain Leddy May.

THE WILD WINDS O' WINTER.

The wild winds o' winter blaw lood through the glen,
An' gane frae the braes are the flo'ers we a' ken ;
The birdies coo'r laigh on ilk bare leafless tree,
An' saut tears are seen where was ance nought but glee.

Noo hush'd is the sang o' the siller-voiced rill,
An' waesome the bleat o' the sheep on the hill;
An' deep lies the snaw, o' what joy can it gie,
When saut tears are seen where was ance nought but glee.

What cauld dule an' sorrow the winter winds bring
To the puir wha in simmer sae licht-herted sing;
For waefu' an' dowie an' warkless they be,
An' saut tears are seen where was ance nought but glee.

There's wee bairnies greetin' wi' bare shilpit feet,
Their claes are nae cleedin' frae cauld blast or sleet;
Oh, wha has a heart that nae pity can gie,
When saut tears are seen where was ance nought but glee.

Oh, ye wha the kind smile o' Fortune hae felt,
A' low to the Fount o' a' blessin's hae knelt,
Wi' kind love in your hearts, oh fear nae to gie,
An' dry the saut tears an' replace them wi' glee.

" 'Tis blessed to gie," sae we're tauld in the Book,
Forbye the deep heart-thanks ane gets in the look
O' them wha receive, as they dry frae their e'e
The saut tears that flow'd where there aye should be glee.

Dear, Faither, we pray, let rich blessin's descen'
On the lo'ed hames o' them wha's kind guidness we ken;
Ne'er let canker'd care wi' cauld blasts clud their e'e.
Nor saut tears be seen where there aye should be glee.

LOVE'S SWEET DREAM.

" Like Dian's kiss, unasked, unsought,
Love gives itself."

LONGFELLOW.

" Avaunt ! to night my heart is light,"
  I will not dream of sorrow,
Though come it may with dawning day
  Upon the new to-morrow.
To-night I'll bathe in those bright eyes,
  That on me now are gleaming ;
With life and love they fill my soul,
  How dear to me their beaming.

No shadow then shall dim my joy,
  While I may thus light-hearted
Drink deep at Love's free-flowing fount,
  Till we must needs be parted.
To clasp her to my beating heart,
  This fair and beauteous maiden,
Clasp her fair form to my poor breast
  So long with sorrow laden.

The joy seems more than I can bear,
  My soul it shall so gladden,
Her heart to feel beat time with mine
  With bliss my brain will madden.
Ah ! Love, thou strange, sweet, mystic spell,
  Com'st thou from some bright Aidenn
To thrill and fill my soul to-night
  With love for this rare maiden.

Or can it be that I but dream,
   Sad, sad would be the waking;
To-night my joy is living bliss,
   To-morrow comes heart-aching.
Never lips my name e'er breathed
   In tones more richly ringing,
Than those that chained me in their power,
   When love came upwards springing.

The miser gloating o'er his gold
   Ne'er felt so rich a feeling.
The drunkard worshipping his wine,
   Or in its madness reeling,
Ne'er knew the pleasure now I know
   In loving this fair maiden—
A maiden true as truth's ownself,
   In yon far distant Aidenn.

To-night this sweet delight is mine—
   To me life's rarest pleasure;
I'll revel in her maiden charms,
   And call her love a treasure;
Could she but ever be to me
   The queen of thought's dominions—
The bride to whom my heart would bow,
   Unscared by false opinions,

To her how proudly would I bow,
   My inmost soul revealing,
And prove through all the years swift gone
   I knew not love's true feeling.

How sweet to drink as now I drink
  Love from her gentle smiling,
And know that carking care and grief
  Are lost through her beguiling.

Dare I but live to love and bliss
  This maiden to me rarest ;
Dare I her gentle brow but kiss,
  My soul deems ever fairest,
This maiden whom my heart adores,
  To-night I feel shall ever
Be as a star of hope to light
  For me life's flowing river.

SONG TO AN EMIGRANT.

While we meet in friendship's circle
  Let our mirth be full and free,
Though we know that we must sever—
  One must cross the deep blue sea ;
Home and kindred leave behind her
  For a far and distant land ;
May this thonght give joy to cheer her :
  Soon she 'll clasp a lov'd one's hand.
    Far away, far away,
      Far away across the sea,
    May the good ship bear thee safely
      To the one so dear to thee.

Far away from dear auld Scotland,
    From the glens and mountains wild,
From the woodlands by the Gala
    Where you rov'd a merry child.
Far away a lov'd one waits thee
    On a strange and foreign strand ;
May life's journey know no sorrows
    As you tread it hand in hand.
      Far away, &c.

May the golden smile of fortune
    Rest upon your happy home,
And may true friends round you gather
    In that land to which you roam.
But forget not your old homeland
    And the friends you leave behind ;
May fond mem'ry oft-times bring them
    Like a sweet dream to your mind.
      Far away, &c.

FREENDSHIP

The hand grasp'd in freendship mair freendly let's grow,
The heart it will lichten when sorrow's streams flow,
I kenna nor carena the warld's cauld froon
If freendship the heart lifts a' sadness aboon.

Why doon in the dumps should we trail owre life's way,
Nor ken o' the lauchter that brichtens the day ;
Though life's brae be steep an' fu' dreary to speel,
Let us fit it richt bauldly an' a' shall be weel.

The smile o' true freendship, oh ! wha wadna ken
The spell that it weaves roond the faint hearts o' men
A fig for braw goud, though to hae it is weel,
Its love o' the freendly gars hearts richer feel.

Your hand then in freendship, you're welcome to mine,
As Time's slippin' by may its spell closer twine,
Till the cludlets o' care frae amangst us depart,
An' the spirit o' freendship reign king owre the heart.

OOR SUNNY DAYS LANGSYNE.

I've wander'd owre oor heather hills in childhood's sunny
    days,
An' through the Haining wuds I've gane in search o' hips
    and slaes ;
Sae merry rang the voices sweet o' lichtsome bairnies
    then— ·
But sunder'd are oor blythesome herts, some far ayont oor
    ken.

Then life was fair, we kent nae care, sic joy the hale day
    lang,
Amang the flo'ers an' birken trees we join'd ilk birdie's
    sang ;
What glorious games enthrall'd us then frae early mornin'
    licht,
Nae callant thocht o' hame ava till fell the cluds o' nicht.

At "fox an' hounds" we scour'd the hills, or den'd in some
    queer place,
Sic awfu' tales we'd sit an' tell while ithers sped the chase;
The "geg" we smuggled then right weel, while time sae
    swiftly flew,
The curfew rang at eicht o'clock e'er ony callant knew.

An' oh! sic fun in winter time when we cam' oot the
    schules,
Sic sclyin' doon the "Auld Brig Road" or on the "Auld
    Brig Pules,"
Or schule 'gainst schule we bauldly focht oor mimic battles
    then,
An' cheer'd oor heroes lood an' lang till foes wad turn an'
    hen.

Sic chairges ilka mother gat to mind an' wake us sune,
When roond the year had brocht that day, the best o' days
    in June,
When in their pride oor burgesses the mairches ride richt
    fast,
An' craftsmen guid, like "Douglas brave" the colours
    deftly cast.

An' weel we mind hoo Johnnie Ha' wad aff-lufe screed
    some sang,
That stirr'd the leal warm herts o' a' to trample doon a
    wrang ;
"The Linglie's Cry" in weel spun verse an' wondrous
    "Water War,"
Recoonted deeds in oor auld toon where Souters fearless
    daur.

The fair days then were thrang-some days, wi' krames an'
    shows galore,
Sic lauchin' an' sic daffin' an' sic rantin' ballads o'er,
Yin scarce could turn aboot ava for Jocks and Jennys
    there,
Whae blythesome socht for maisters new whom they micht
    ser' wi' care.

But O that loon, Auld Time, gangs roond, an' sunders far
    and wide,
The blythe wee bairns that play'd langsyne by Ettrick's
    wimplin' tide ;
Yet in the gloamin' oors we see their faces ain an' a',
An' in oor dreams their voices sweet like music owre us fa'.

Oor ain auld toon, we lo'e thee yet, rich blessin's on thy
    name,
Like ivy to the sturdy tree oor hert clings to its hame—
Where first we saw sweet beauty bloom on haughs an'
    bonny braes,
An' pleasure's smile illumed wi' bliss oor life's bricht sunny
    days.

WELCOME SPRING.

Air—" O, are ye sleepin', Maggie."

———

When wild the winter breezes blaw
   Thro' the woodlands dark an' eerie,
An' a' aroond lies driftin' snaw,
   The blithest heart grows unco drearie.
      O, Spring, ye're welcome, fu' o' smilin',
      O, Spring, ye're welcome, fu' o' smilin',
      To glad the earth wi' joyous birth,
      An' ilka heart frae care beguilin'.

Sweet Spring has gently changed the scene,
   An' flo'ers begin to grow fu' bonnie ;
Ilk lo'esome lassie trysts at e'en,
   She'll meet and wander wi' her Johnnie.

Nae mair, nae mair wi' cheeks fu' blae
   We'll dowie hing oot owre the ingle,
An' langin', sigh Jock Frost wad gae,
   Wha mak's the ears an' fingers tingle.

Noo glints the sun wi' cheerin' beams,
   An' openin' buds bedeck the timmer,
The warblin' birds an' wimplin' streams
   Foretell the joys o' gouden simmer.

BAIRNIE SAE FAIR.

AIR—" Robin Adair."

Nane like yoursel' we see,
   Bairnie sae fair ;
Cam' ye frae lands on hie,
   Bairnie sae fair ?
Mou' fu' o' kisses sweet,
Though we search ilka street
Like thee nae ane we'll meet,
   Bairnie sae fair.

Lauchter sae rich and free,
   Bairnie sae fair,
Like music fa's frae thee,
   Bairnie sae fair ;
Joy to ilk heart it brings,
Love's spell roond a' it flings,
Care speeds on fleetin' wings—
   Bairnie sae fair.

Jewels fu' brightly shine,
   Bairnie sae fair ;
Nane like thy een sae fine,
   Bairnie sae fair ;
Dauted sweet darlin' wee,
Dearer than a' to me,
Pure may thy life aye be,
   Bairnie sae fair.

H

LOVE'S TRYST IN YARROW.

When simmer busket a' oor hills,
An' blythely sang the siller rills,
While lav'rocks pour'd their lo'esome trills
　　　Aboon the braes o' Yarrow.
Young Jamie vow'd he wad be seen
Row'd in his plaid at dewy e'en
Amang the heather wi' his Jean—
　　　The fairest maid in Yarrow.

His tryst he kept, the lassie fair
Wi' smiles o' welcome met him there,
Hearts fu' o' love, they ken nae care
　　　Amang the braes o' Yarrow.
Pure as the dewdrap on the bell
That beauty lends to hill an' dell,
The words o' love sae sweetly fell
　　　On Jeanie's ears in Yarrow.

Nae dreams o' grandeur touch'd their hearts
Nor learn'd were they in Fashion's arts,
They answered but to Cupid's darts
　　　Amang the braes o' Yarrow.
Young Jeanie syne gied her consent,
Ere lies the snaw upon the bent
Mess John frae Selkirk will be sent
　　　To tie love's knot in Yarrow.

THE MINSTREL'S GANE.

Robert Crosbie, born at Darnick, 1821; Died at Innerleithen, 1891.

AIR—"Memories Dear.'

———

By the ingle-side sitting come dreams o' sweet childhood,
  The days o' langsyne, when life's pleasures were fair,
When rich rang the sangs o' the birds thro' the wild wood,
  Nor thocht we o' grief that makes the heart sair.
Sae joyous I wander'd till deep fell the gloamin',
  An' sank the red sun owre the hills, far away,
Then hameward returnin', sae tired oot wi' roamin',
  I'd sink into rest, and I'd dream o' sweet play;
          Dear dreams o' life's morn.

Sae weel do l mind in oor auld toon o' meetin'
  The true freends I've lo'ed sin' the days o' langsyne;
Their bricht smiles I see on fancy's wings fleetin',
  Their kind words I'll treasure while life's star is mine.
'Twas then that I met wi' the kind minstrel, Robin,
  Wha sang like the linties that lilt owre the braes;
But noo he has finished life's sair tangl'd bobbin;
  His harp it is hush'd, and he'll sing nae mair lays,
          Nor dream o' life's morn.

Hoo sweetly he sang o' his ain bonnie Mary,
  And the joys they had felt 'neath the "auld beechen tree;"
'Mid the "pleasures o' spring," ilk blythe as a fairy,
  By lo'ed "Darnick Burn" they wad wander wi' glee.

But hush'd is the harp, for the minstrel lies sleepin'
    The still sleep o' death by the Leithen's green braes ;
We'll whiles think o' Robin, tho' time's owre us creepin',
    An' whiles to his mem'ry we'll croon his sweet lays,
              'Mid dreams o' life's morn.

Life's years fade and dee like the flo'ers o' the simmer
    That brichten earth's scenes till cauld blast blaw fu' drear;
Like leaves drappin' sear frae the ance bonnie timmer,
    Time bears us away frae the scenes that are dear.
Oh ! let us be mindfu' there's joy that's supernal,
    Forever it bides 'yont the bricht sky on hie,
Where gouden harps ring thro' the ages eternal,
    Oh ! wha wadna wish 'mid sic glory to be,
             'Yont dreams o' life's morn.

TILL THE STAR OF LIFE SHALL WANE.

AIR—" When the Roses Come Again."

I will linger in the gloaming,
    Where the shadows love to play ;
Where, in life's bright, golden morning,
    Hand in hand we used to stray.
Not a care, nor pang of sorrow
    Dimm'd the beauty of your eye ;
Then I lov'd, but we were parted ;
    Darling, can you tell me why ?
          Till the star of life shall wane,
          Till the star of life shall wane ;
        I will love thee, oh ! my darling,
          Till the star of life shall wane.

I will linger in the gloaming
  'Neath the dear old chestnut tree,
Where the birds would mate in spring time,
  And I dreamt to mate with thee.
And still dreaming, Love, is asking—
  But my heart can only sigh—
Must we live life's years still parted ;
  Darling, can your heart reply ?
        Till the star of life shall wane, &c.

I will linger in the gloaming
  Till the shadows die away,
And the night shall hide for ever
  All the fleeting hours of day.
I will watch and wait your coming
  Till the angels bright draw nigh,
Then we'll meet and ne'er be parted,
  Darling, in that land on high.
        Till the star of life shall wane,
        Till the star of life shall wane ;
      I will love thee, oh ! my darling,
        Till the star of life shall wane.

DREAMINGS OF YARROW.

'Tis many and many a year ago
  When the youthful spirit was free,
In the golden glow of the summer sun
  That I wander'd so oft with thee.
And never a thought of the after years
  Would e'er pierce the heart with sorrow,
As we stray'd in the morn or dewy eve
  Through the dowie dens of Yarrow.

Ah ! then, there was joy and laughter sweet
  In the beautiful vale so fair,
And the scented flowers by the river's brink
  Bow'd their heads with the sighing air.
While hymning in joy to the bright blue sky,
  The lark we watch'd in its gladness ;
But oft would we ask why such silence reigns,
  Dwells here the spirit of sadness ?

And lo ! at the eve in the sunset's glow,
  While the shadows of night descend,
As if bound in chains, that were weirdly strange,
  Our homeward way slowly we'd wend,
And dreams, sweet dreams, in our sleep would come,
  Fill'd with many a green-clad fairy,
Who chanted the music of the stream
  That flows from the lone St. Mary.

The brightness of youth oft fades like the mists
   That rise from the hills at the morn,
And the void heart is left all sear'd and rent
   Like the bush by the wild winds torn.
Like the sun's last rays are the joys that are fled ;
   But why all this sad, sad sorrow,
Or dreams of those years 'mid a mist of tears,
   With sighs like the winds in Yarrow.

Oh ! hopes of youth like the clouds flitting by
   As curtains light hung on the air,
They are ours but a while, then dying down,
   Leave the heart but the haunt of care.
Though true love is sweet, yet tender the spell
   That breaks in the dawn of sorrow,
Like eddies that circle and outward spread
   In the deep, deep pools of Yarrow.

TO MRS AGNES S. MABON, JEDBURGH.

AUTHOR OF "HOMELY RHYMES," &c.

I hae read wi' heartfelt pleasure
   The liltin's o' your lyre,
An' I vow ilk weel set measure
   Can touch the heart wi' fire.
Nae fusionless, sad carpin's,
   But sweet, sweet notes o' sang,
They thrill the soul that's weary,
   And gar it feel fu' strang.

Ken ye my spirit feels richt prood
   That poesy's been led,
To wander through oor Borderland
   And dwell by crystal Jed.
Fair bowers o' love and beauty,
   Where fancy sweet may dream,
Are biggit on its flower-clad banks,
   Where sang-gems brichtly gleam,

There simmer grandly glowin' comes
   Wi' strange and mystic spell,
While the feather'd bards o' nature
   Ilk wild note richly swell.
Nae wonder ye hae caught and caged
   Within your ain wee hoose
A bonnie, warblin' lintie bird
   That sings sae kind and croose.

Lang may your lintie trill its notes,
   Sic sangs sink in the heart,
And wake the depths o' manhood up
   To bear life's nobler part.
And lang may love and guidness croon
   The sweet joys o' your hame,
While oor ain mither Scotland owns
   Your weel won poet name.

THE YOUNG MEN WE MEET.

"Fools, fools all of them, where are your wise men?"

———

Of all the young men in our town east or west
The masher is known by the way he is dress'd
By the style of his hair and the pipe that he smokes,
By his " hums " and his " haws " and the stalest of jokes,

How he struts in his pride away down the street,
A thing to be proud of, a dandie complete ;
In the swing of his stick or his iv'ry top'd cane
There is proof that of self he's uncommonly vain.

See what a display on the front of his vest,
Of bright shining gold—he says 'tis the best ;
And rings three or four on his fingers he's too,
With a flourish so fine he will bring them in view.

And how jolly he laughs as he struts and he stares
With his newest style hat just stuck on three hairs ;
Was there ever a one—go search up and down—
Who can ape better yet the fun-raising clown.

The glass he can swill, calls drink nectar divine,
And fits himself well for the comp'ny of swine ;
Like a trooper he swears, be sure he can speak,
Though the deep blush of shame may oft mantle the cheek.

He ogles the maids with a smirk and a smile,
Who are silly enough to be caught with his guile ;
Oh a dandie is he, go measure him well,
And the weight of his brain you quickly may tell.

Oh the masher is good and the masher is true,
Yet the maiden he weds how quick must she rue,
The path she has chosen to tread through this life—
'Tis a pathway of tears and of unending strife.

For a coward is he and a dastard to boot
Who acts out his love with his fist and his foot,
Then sing of heart feelings, with pathos sublime,
Our poets have sung in the grandest of rhyme.

Now don't shake your head and cry stop, that's enough,
'Tis the vilest of nonsense and right arrant stuff,
Yet the masher we sing of and such of his kind
'Mongst the thousands we meet in our own town we find.

Yes, he acts and he speaks as if life were a jest
And man a machine to be fed and fine dress'd,
With never a soul to be fitted through love
For the presence of God in the Kingdom above.

As if hell's but a fable, an old fashion'd tale
To frighten the weak as they pass through life's vale,
But truth it shall stand like the name of our God,
And this they shall feel when shall fall His dread rod.

To true heights of manhood may each seek to grow,
Nor fear we to ease fellow mortals of woe;
'Tis noble, 'tis God-like, live life's golden rule,
Nor pass through this vale as though born but a fool.

OOR TEDDY.

We hae a laddie a' oor ain,
In a' the toon like him there's nane,
A bonnie, sweet, wee darling wean—
    Sae winsome is oor Teddy.
      Teddy has a bricht blue e'e,
        Sprightly Teddy, restless Teddy ;
      Teddy's stown my heart frae me—
        Nae bairn can match wi' Teddy.

He hauds the hoose in sic a steer
Wi' antic tricks an' mischief queer,
Yet to ilk heart the rogie's dear—
    O pawkie is oor Teddy.

The bairns maun wi' him a' thing share,
For he is maister, aye, an' mair ;
He dings them aff baith stule and chair—
    Nae peace get they wi' Teddy.

He keeks sae slee into my face
If froon or anger he can trace,
If nane, then lauchter fills the place—
    An' unco loon is Teddy.

Oh ! blessings on oor bairnie wee,
Aye cosh and canty may he be—
Frae a' the wiles o' sorrow free
    Through life be thou, oor Teddy.

THE SWEETEST FLO'ER O' A.'

Sae bonnie are the flo'ers that bloom alang the braes,
Enrichin' Nature's dress in simmer's gouden days ;
But bonnie though they be an' charms aroond us thraw,
Oh I ken o' a flower that's sweeter than them a'.

    Oh bonnie lassie, dainty lassie,
      When the gloamin' haps the glen
    Then we shall wander, blythely wander,
      Through the woods where nane may ken.

When saft winds kiss the hills an' Gala's murmurin' stream
Then fancy oft-times roves in love's enthrallin' dream,
An' wild birds trill their notes while gloamin' shadows fa',
But gie to me the voice that's sweeter than them a'.

    Oh ! bonnie lassie, &c.,

CANNY GAUN TAM.

Air—" Imph—m."

I've wander'd aboot in my life sirs awee,
An' a' kinds o' fouk hae aft met my e'e ;
But o' a' the queer chiels that across my path cam',
Nae ane could compare wi' canny gaun Tam.

Chorus.

Oh, canny gaun Tam, yes, canny gaun Tam,
The plague o' oor place is canny gaun Tam ;
He's mair o' a mule than a sweet temper'd lamb,
Ne'er saw ye the like o' canny gaun Tam.

Wad he dae for the " force ? ' juist gae look an' see,
A man o' " true blue " I think he'd fain be
Owre some beggar ta'en in, the Bailie's he'd cram,
Till jail'd they wad be through canny gaun Tam.

Nae mou's hauf like his in a' the hale toon,
His face it micht mak' a gude harvest moon,
His feet maybe ser' for a batt'rin' ram,
E'er saw ye the like o' canny gaun Tam.

The bairns jook the corners an' lauchin' they cry—
" What's he daein', hey ! " the muckle dunce spy,
Nae bummies he'll catch hoo e'er he ram-stam,
Sic a muckle saft lump is canny gaun Tam.

Gin ye tell him " dae this," he's sure to dae " that,"
A sumph he's been ca'd, wi' heid like a pat ;
But say what ye like he'll keep unco calm,
He kens what is best for canny gaun Tam.

As to wha he maun be, I ken ye'll a' speir
Gin he's in oor toon or onywhere near,
But tak' ye my word that he is nae sham,
Gae ask at yoursel', " ken I canny gaun Tam ? "

IMOGENE.

" You are not wrong who deem
'Tis but a dream within a dream."

E. A. Poe.

In the calm and silent night,
In the soft sweet dawning light,
  Imogene I dream of thee—
With thy bright and star-like eyes,
Lit with life that never dies,
Eyes that speak in glad surprise—
  Words of faith and love to me.

And I give thee all my heart.
Give it all and not a part,
Maiden free from coquette's art
  Love and claim me as thine own.
As I watch thy maiden grace,
Watch the beauty of thy face
  Where the light of truth is shown.

I would clasp thee maiden fair
With the long soft auburn hair,
Clasp thee close thou lov'd one rare,
  Maiden of such matchless grace
  In a fond and warm embrace.

And thus dreaming I arise
With fond pleading in my eyes
  And advancing, love, to thee ;
With my arms outstretch'd to clasp—
Outstretch'd in love thus to grasp
  Form of beauty dear to me.

Then I stop with sudden thrill,
My whole heart and pow'r of will
Startled thus is almost still,
  And one step I cannot move,
Though thy sweet, thy winning smile,
Free from all the world's guile,
  Fills my heart and soul with love.

Like the sun's effulgent gleam
Shining on the dancing stream
  Is the bright glance of thine eyes,
  Purer than the azure skies,
  Pure as life that never dies,
How I revel in Love's dream.

Then the dawning of the light
Chasing out the shades of night,
Driving out the murky gloom
From the corner of the room
  Pictures forth, oh, maiden fair,
  Eyes and smiles and auburn hair.

Beauteous maiden, Imogene,
Maiden whom I've claim'd as mine,
  Stepping there so trim and neat,
  Stepping light on fairy feet,
Then receding from my view
Like a phantom all untrue.
  Thou art gone, oh vision sweet !
  Here again no more to meet.
Gone, alas ! fair lov'd one mine,
Like, a dream, sweet Imogene.

THE PAUPER'S LOT.

[Pausing in front of a large English Workhouse to have a look at it,
the great, heavy gates swung open, and at a quick pace issued
forth the lonely, grim, grey workhouse hearse—it was a pauper's
funeral.]

Jerry along
With one horse strong
Why there's none to say us nay,
For life is fled,
A pauper's dead,
We'll bury him just to-day.

'Mid ceaseless woe,
God wot we know,
He trode life's jogging round ;
We'll ply the whip,
With crack and flip,
And he'll soon be in the ground.

A six-foot grave,
With grudge they gave,
They said " more than good for him ;"
But here he goes,
Free from earth's woes
In a shell that's grey and grim.

For such folks dead
No tears are shed,
A wretch whom none could love ;
On to the grave
The parish gave,
We'll land him safe with a shove.

Jerry, my boys,
Nor heed the noise
Pace off at a good sharp trot;
With spade in hand
The sextons stand
To show us the pauper's lot.

Ah! whence that tear
Dropp'd on his bier,
Did it fall from angels' eyes?
Where bright hosts stand
In His fair land,
And never a pauper dies.

THE HEART'S BEST GIFT

What shall I give to my beautiful one?
Something to keep forever and aye;
A something the heart can treasure and own
Till the death mists shall close o'er life's day.

Say, shall it be but some fanciful gift,
Nor its value the price of a toy
That gleams in the light of the clouds' broad rift,
That the earth rust may quickly destroy.

Ah, no! the gift to my beautiful one,
It must be what the fond heart well knows
Fades not like the sun when the day is done,
But from strength unto strength ever grows.

I

Love, nothing but love, whole hearted and true
　To my beautiful one I shall give,
Though life's gifts be few, my lot I'll ne'er rue,
　In the light of her smile I shall live.

BURNS.

A manly peasant, marked with clay, rough-shod for honest
　　toil,
Was he who flung upon the gale rich songs that round us
　　coil :
Rich spells of sweet enthralling power that burst the chains
　　of care,
And waked to glorious joyousness souls drifting to despair.

Immortal Burns ! the deathless song pour'd from thy harp's
　　rich string
Till hill and vale, and lands afar with its rare music ring,
And manhood draws a deeper breath of freedom's purer air,
And hearts to love's sweet thrill awake where beauty
　　blooms so fair.

Fond fancy in her fleeting dreams treads o'er each scene
　　to-day
By gurgling Ayr and bonnie Doon, where oft the bard
　　would stray ;
And eyes grow dim with flowing tears by Highland Mary's
　　grave,
Whose ling'ring star shall never set while beats the storm-
　　toss'd wave.

And there the ancient haunted kirk, where death was
    thought to keep
The crumbling dust laid in repose from passions wild and deep;
Ne'er lightnings flash'd o'er such a scene as met Tam's
    dazzled eye
When forth the throng of witches poured the grey mare's
    pace to try.

And reverential would we kneel beside the cottar's hearth,
And with the sage pour forth heart-praise to Him who
    rules the earth.
My country, bless'd indeed wert thou did love for God but
    reign,
Nor hypocritic, canting talk thy sons and daughters stain.

And surging fast rolls life's red tide as though we dared
    the fray,
When rings old Scotland's battle-hymn—heart-thrilling
    " Scots wha hae."
Was never land more bless'd than ours—the free land of
    the brave,
Where blooms the daisy " crimson tipp'd " and rough burr
    thistles wave.

Oh, glorious sight!   See, song-entranced the many thousands
    stand,
Who, travel-stain'd, as pilgrims come to dear loved Scotia's
    strand ;
And, bending bare-brow'd o'er the dust of him no true heart
    spurns,
They bless the hour that gave to earth the gifted minstrel
    Burns.

DEAR LAND, FARE THEE WELL.
Inscribed to 1. B.

Land of grandeur, though I leave thee,
O'er all lands thou'rt loved, believe me ;
Each heath-glad hill and winding dell
Twines round the heart a mystic spell
That ne'er shall break nor fade and die,
While beams the light in beauty's eye.
Scotland, land of rill and river—
Homeland, I'll forget thee never.
   Dear old Scotland, beauty's fair land ;
   Brave old Scotland, freedom's rare land ;
   The home of love's enchanting spell
   With sadden'd heart we bid farewell.

Land of beauty, though I leave thee,
And a foreign strand receive me
Far distant o'er the darkling sea,
Yet still my heart shall cling to thee :
Home of childhood, ever fairest,
Land where love finds all that's rarest ;
Old Scotland, land where freedom dwells
'Mid tow'ring hills and bosky dells.

Land of grandeur, while I leave thee,
Know that partings ever grieve me ;
When beyond the restless ocean,
True hearts lov'd with warm devotion,

As though I wandered still o'er thee,
In dreams of fancy oft I'll see,
Old Scotland, land of moor and fell,
The sails are set, " Good night—farewell."
 Dear old Scotland, beauty's fair land ;
 Brave old Scotland, freedom's rare land ;
 The home of love's enchanting spell
 With sadden'd heart we bid farewell.

BIRTHDAY GREETINGS.

Hail to thee, dear to me, beautiful May,
Sing we with joy of thy brightening ray,
Telling the tempests of Winter are o'er,
Gone are Spring's chilling blasts, gone from our shore
Hail to the flowers thou'st brought in thy train,
Springing to gladden the hill and the plain,
Coming as messengers full of sweet love,
Sent by our Father God dwelling above.
Joyous indeed be our friend's natal day,
Thrice welcome with thee, oh ! beautiful May.

Hail to thee, dear to me, beautiful May,
Driving the gloom and the dark mists away ;
How sparkling and bright are the swift bounding streams
Laughing in song 'neath the sun's golden beams.

Hark, all the woodlands are ringing with song,
Weariness past, now the heart groweth strong ;
Burden'd with blesssings thrice welcome we sing
Coming to thee, friend, on Time's fleeting wing,
Type may it be of God's own perfect day,
Thine own natal month, bright beautiful May.

WHAT'S A' THE STEER ABOOT.

Epistle to W. N., Selkirk.

Your hand, man, Willie, canty chiel,
Wi' a' my heart I wish ye weel ;
While you an' yours spin life's queer reel
     Till ends its tether,
Yours health, an' meat, an' cosy biel',
     My rhymin' brither.

Haith, sic a steer auld Scotland's in, sic sighin' an' sad
     moanin',
Ilk fitfu' blast wafts them away owre hill an' dark, drear
     loanin' ;
Nor ingles bleeze wi' cheery blink, an' lauchter's seldom
     ringin',
But, like the dew in sweet May-time, the pearly teardraps
     hingin'.

The widespread 'plaint frae guidwives is—" Oh, that the
    wark was better,
Then we'd thank God wi' a' oor hearts an' be to nae man
    debtor."
An' dowiely ilk guidman looks ; but wha can tell ilk feelin'
That rankles deeply in the heart an' sets him maist mad
    reelin' ?

Strong-limb'd an' fu' o' health, an' yet he's helpless as a
    bairnie,
While some will meanly, sneerin' cry, " For wark ma man
    ye carena."
But where's the wark ?   The heart, the hand are mair than
    ever willin'
To toil a' through the langsome day to win an honest
    shillin'.

There's a weary sough I dinna like in the blasts roond
    Meigle sweepin',
An' hungry bairns—God keep them a'—by the cauldrife
    hearths are creepin' :
Oor braw wee bairns, life's richest joys, when simmer days
    are bonnie
Their lauchter sweet, like lav'rocks' sangs, wad cheer the
    hearts o' ony.

It's weel for fouk that kenna want an' dream but o' star-
    vation,
But, hech ! that pride, that Christless pride they hedge
    aroond their station,

It makes them heartless; dinna touch the goud that lines
 their pockets—
Like drawin' life-bluid frae their hearts, or richt airms frae
 their sockets.

We're made o' but ae flesh an' bluid, ae common form that's
 human—
We're sprung frae ae guid faither man an' weel-lo'ed mither
 woman.
"That's false," thus whispers selfish pride; " yon, starvin'
 wretch, my brither ?
It canna be; I'd claim him not were there on earth nae
 ither."

Cauld moanin' winds, how drearily they gar us start an'
 shiver,
An' we dream o' hame an' hamely joys we pray may last
 forever :
Strange changes Time brings aft aboot—the rich, the puir
 change places ;
May God's wheels, grindin' slow but sure, grind into a' His
 graces.

Then wad the sair-heart cry widespread nae mair ring
 through our valleys,
Nor wad we hear the bitter curse breath'd forth that makes
 men callous ;
But love—yes, God-like love wad reign o'er warld's cares
 supernal,
An' peace—heart-sighed for peace, would come rich laden
 frae the Eternal.

But, ah ! I doot that dream's owre sweet while some grip
    hard the gear, man,
As though 'twere theirs—a gouden key to earth an' heaven
    sae dear, man ;
Though honest puir they'd fearless starve an' ban them for
    their moanin' :
God grant that fortune's smile will beam in ilka weel-kent
    loanin'.

I'LL AYE BE TRUE.

I'll no gang through the wud, mither,
    Nor by the auld beech tree,
Where in the gloamin' lassies gang
    Their ain true luves to see.

I winna wander by the burn,
    Nor owre yon bonnie brae,
Where bloom sweet flo'ers o' ilka hue
    An' birds sing a' the day.

I'll no gang by the ha', mither,
    Though its sae braw to see,
For when I meet the laird himsel'
    He aye mak's luve to me.

An' surely ye maun ken, mither,
   The lad I lo'e sae weel
Is far ayont the saut, saut sea
   Wi' hert aye warm an' leal.

I doot my hert wad break, mither,
   I ken I'd dwine an' dee,
If after a', my pure true luve,
   The lad pruv'd fause to me.

But no, I canna doot, mither,
   That braw, braw lad sae true,
Wha pledged his ain guid word o' faith
   Me only he wad lo'e.

An' sune the day will dawn, mither,
   He'll mak' me his guidwife,
An' happiness will croon oor hame
   Through a' oor days in life.

Sae let the laird gae by, mither,
   He'll no be lo'ed by me,
Though braw his ha' I'll aye be true
   To him that's owre the sea.

OOR JAMIE.

Losh, where is oor wee Jamie gane,
    He's oot amang the weans ;
I doot the rogue is daein' wrang—
    Aye, there he's thrawin' stanes.
Sirce me ! the bairns aboot the place,
    Some bigger than himsel',
Are fear'd when Jamie joins their games,
    For lood he makes them yell.

Come in this meenit, Jamie, come—
    He's gane juist like a deer ;
Hear hoo he lauchs, he heads na me,
    Gin I but had him here,
I'd let him ken—but there he's fa'n
    An' clour'd his bonnie broo,
My ain wee man, let's kiss the place ?
    There, there it's better noo.

Man, Jamie, stop—aweel juist gang,
    I canna sae ye nae,
Though but frae mischief ye wad keep
    Ye'd get mair oot to play.
Richt weel I ken your sweet blue een,
    An' that wee prattlin' mou'
Twines roond my heart an' makes me laugh
    At muckle that ye do.

Gude grant my ain braw little son,
  That ye'll be spared to me,
An' as ye grow to man's estate
  Frae mischief keep ye free.
May my ain son defend the richt,
  Nor bend to deeds o' shame,
But keep, aye keep, the causey croon
  Wi' pure an' spotless name.

IN MEMORIAM—OOR JAMIE.

BORN MARCH 26TH, 1876. DIED JANUARY 26TH, 1890.

Oor hearts are sair to pairt wi' you,
  Oor laddie lo'ed sae dear,
For weel we ken we never mair
  On earth your step shall hear ;
An' O, to think at oor hearthstane
  The voice o' sang is still—
That voice that sang o' Christ's great love
  Oor hearts wi' joy to fill.

Oor hearts, though sair, rejoice to ken
  'Tis but a wee, wee while
We'll tread the lanely path o' life,
  Then we'll meet Jamie's smile ;

An' bendin' at the Golden Throne,
 We'll " Worship Christ the King,"
Wha's blood was shed on Calv'ry's cross,
 To us sic joys to bring.

Though pairtins here are sair to bear,
 We'll lean on Jesus' breast,
'Tis there we find sweet balm for grief—
 Ay ! there alane there's rest.
The dear anes ca'd away frae earth
 Are but sweet links abune
That draw us hame to pairt nae mair
 When life on earth is dune.

THE STEERIN' WEAN.

Where in ony toon or parish is there sic a steerin' wean ?
Braw rosy cheeks an' lauchin' een has this lassie a' oor ain.
Hear her crawin' unco crously, mischief shinin' in ilk e'e,
What a warld o' pleasure is there in that darlin' wean to me.

No' ae meenit will she quiet sit upon her mither's knee ;
Watch her noo, hoo hard she sprauchles a' her fecht's to
 get to me.
Noo she's canty—what a lassie— tryin' to get at my hair ;
Frae oot my pouch the wee tick-tick she is puin' fell an
 sair.

Listen to the wee man chappin' sticks as hard as e'er he can ;
What ? ye want to see him workin' ; that, I'm sure, he
    wadna stan'.
Doon again, she's after pussie, tryin' hard her tail to pu',
But the pussie kens oor lassie, an' she's rinnin' frae her noo.

Losh ! she's got the muckle poker ; there, she's hurt her
    handie wee,
An' I doot that sleep is tryin' noo to close ilk sparklin' e'e.
What a wark she gi'es her mither, a' the day frae morn to
    nicht,
No a meenit's peace or quiet, aft wi' her we get a fricht.

Noo she's sleepin', bonnie lassie, she's as soun' as soun' can
    be,
There is nane in a' the warld that can charm my heart like
    thee.
Blythesome bairnie, restin' sweetly, this shall ever be oor
    pray'r—
That oor Faither aye will guard thee, keep thee ever pure
    an' fair.

THE STANDARD OF STUART.

AIR—"Flora Macdonald's Lament."

The standard that rose in Glenfinnan's green vale
  Sank bloody and torn on Culloden's red field :
The loud voice of triumph rang wild on the gale—
  For tyranny won o'er the claymore and shield.
The true and the brave now may fly o'er the ocean,
  The shieling that knew them shall know them no more ;
And the maidens who loved with the fondest devotion,
  In sorrow may weep on the shell-girded shore:
The song and the dance, where the heather-bells wave,
Are things of the past since the death of the brave.

As firm as the rock of their own native Highlands,
  That's swept by the tempest that rides o'er the main,
Prov'd dauntless the sons of the mainland and islands,
  Who never shall list to the pibroch again.
The dun deer shall browse where once stood the lov'd shieling,
  The moor-fowl shall nest where the lovers would meet ;
And truth, like the winds, comes around us, soft stealing,
  Foretelling that Stuarts as kings we'll ne'er greet :
Their star it has set in the depth of the grave,
And no more o'er our land shall their standard e'er wave.

The death-dirge is wail'd for the chieftans so true,
  Who lived in the love of their clansmen so brave ;
They're gone from our midst, and their absence we rue,
  Since their homes now resound to the stranger and slave.

Woe, woe to our land, should the foe e'er annoy her ;
   The red rust lies thick on the claymore and shield ;
Soon, soon might the foe in his madness destroy her,
   Since gone are the brave who were fear'd on the field :
Their shielings are wreck'd by the hand of the slave—
Like the standard of Stuart, gone, gone are the brave.

DOON THE DELL.

Come wi' me when fa's the gloamin',
   Let us wander doon the dell,
Wrapp'd within my cosy plaidie
   Fain to thee I'd " something " tell.
Witchin' charms ye've cast around me,
   Closer still I feel them twine,
Till my heart wi' warm emotion
   Whispers " Lassie, I am thine."

There's a wealth o' love an' beauty
   In the beamin' o' ye'r e'e
That has made me feel nae lassie
   Can be half sae dear as thee.
Life to me would be as naething,
   Save a ceaseless sea o' care,
Were thy voice and glance denied me,
   And thy form sae matchless fair.

Doon the dell where sweet the burnie
   Wimples blythely on its way,
Doon the dell where ilka birdie
   Lilts its ain kind lo'esome lay.
Come, dear lassie, dinna linger,
   Hear the distant e'enin' bell
Peal the hour ye trysted wi' me,
   We wad wander down the dell.

AULD SCOTLAND'S GLORIOUS THREE.

(WALLACE, BRUCE, AN' BURNS.)

Hail, dear auld Scotland! through my veins
   The warm blood flows wi' pride,
An' leaps my heart to ken in thee
   Fair Freedom maun reside.
Nor craven-hearted are the sons
   Sprung frae brave sons o' thine,
Thou land o' Wallace, Bruce, an' Burns,
   Prood names in Fame's fair shrine.

When England dared wi' haughty mein
   Tyrannic might to show,
An' scorned the voice o' warnin' gi'en,
   Nor stemm'd the tide o' woe ;

K

Then Wallace, lion-hearted knight,
  Wi' guid claymore an' shield,
Crushed in his pride proud Cressingham
  On Stirling's blood-stain'd field.

An' how ilk Scottish heart was thrill'd
  An' scorned the thocht o' truce
When England's hosts at Bannockburn
  Were met by Robert Bruce ;
The kingli'st king e'er Scotland knew,
  By ae decisive stroke,
Shrined Freedom in our native land
  An' burst the tyrant's yoke.

An' wha thus born 'neath freedom's skies
  But hated wrang aye spurns,
Thrice welcomes wi' a heart o' love
  The lays o' Robert Burns.
Brave soul'd an' true, nae man he fear'd,
  But sang, strang-voiced an' fine,
O' " Scots Wha Hae," an' " Afton's Stream,"
  An' dear-lo'ed " Auld Langsyne."

Oh, glorious three, what patriot heart
  But dear hauds ilk ken'd name,
An' Time but proves how bricht they shine
  Upon the scroll o' fame.
For Freedom, Worth, an' Minstrelsy
  Ilk wears a star-gem'd croon,
An' he wha daurs to scorn their names
  He's but a witless loon.

But dauntless yet the Scottish heart,
 Where'er it beats on earth,
Still clings to Scotland wi' leal love—
 The fair land o' oor birth.
An' while the thistle wags its head
 An' heather croons the hill,
The names o' Wallace, Bruce, an' Burns
 The Scottish patriot thrill.

TENDER AND TRUE.

Oh, to be thrill'd by the love of a fair one,
 Oh, but to watch for the glance of her eye,
Oh, but to catch the lov'd song from her ripe lips
 Ere it pass on the winds that are whisp'ring by.
Bright as the summer hours life must be ever
 When the heart's chain'd in love's blissful spell,
Reaping the gladness that's free from all sorrow,
 Laughter and joy in love's home ever dwell.
  Murmuring softly, gently, and sweetly—
   Ever to thee I'll be tender and true ;
  Love passes not like the wanton winds fleetly,
   Only to thee I'll be tender and true.

Oh, to be stirr'd when we meet with a rare one,
   Oh, but to know the rich spell of her smile,
Oh, but to stay where her presence would cheer one,
   Twining and binding the heart in love's coil.
It makes the heart dance, the charm of her beauty,
   Nothing we find with her brightness can vie,
Faultless eyes gleaming, still in her bosom
   Reign feelings that speak in love's tenderest sigh.
     Murmuring softly, gently, and sweetly—
      Ever to thee I'll be tender and true ;
     Love passes not like the wanton winds fleetly
      Only to thee I'll be tender and true.

WHAT LIVES ?

Along the corridors of Time Life walks with ceaseless
    tread :
To-day we're marching with the throng, to-morrow with the
    dead.
Kings, princes, lords, and sons of toil eat, sleep, and work
    or play ;
A laugh, a song, one heart-beat, and then they sink in,
    death's decay.

To-day we bridge the world o'er, or span the restless **deep**,
Man's voice can reach earth's farthest bounds, his **thoughts**
     the mountains leap.
He grasps the earth as 'twere a toy, and who can say him
     nay ;
He seeks its mines, robs them of wealth, then sinks in
     death's decay.

Man breathes the wondrous gift of God, and wakes his
     thrilling song
Till the music of his song-gift stirs the ever-moving throng,
And the beating of their hearts with his measure seems to
     sway
Through life's morning and its noon—till they sink in
     death's decay.

See, see across the mighty deep in triumph how he rides—
A stately ship and a fearless heart the world's vast
     commerce guides.
Within our marts how proud he pours earth's produce day
     by day ;
Earth's fruits he gives, earth's wealth he gains, then sinks
     in death's decay.

A kingly crown man's brow adorns, a nation lists his words,
In marshall'd ranks up spring the brave, forth flash a
     million swords ;
With haughty mein his will commands, who dares to
     disobey
He scorns, he hates, promotes, degrades, then sinks in
     death's decay.

The densest forest cannot hide their secrets from his eyes,
Through patient, persevering skill he wins the world's prize.
On Afric's darkness pours the light with ever-bright'ning
      ray ;
Then feted, honour'd by the crowd, he sinks in death's
      decay.

What lives ? 'tis ask'd in whispers, and with loud and eager
      voice :
God's glorious work through frail, weak man, oh, let your
      heart rejoice—
A vessel for the King of Kings made meet for endless day,
To prove His power and hold the gem that knows not
      death's decay.

FRIENDSHIP'S INVITATION.

Inscribed to a City Friend.

Come when morn with beauty glowing,
   Gilds the hills, the glens, the lea,
By fair Tweed in richness flowing
   I would wander there with thee.

Oft in fancy I am straying
   Down the well-remember'd glade,
Where thy harp-strings sweet spells playing
   Made us friends, fair minstrel maid.

Hasten, minstrel, in thy brightness !
  Meet once more by Tweed's rare stream ;
Let me hear thy footstep's lightness,
  Let us watch those bright eyes gleam.

Oft thy voice in softness stealing
  Falls like music on my ear,
Till from dreams I wake, revealing
  Only dreams have brought thee near.

Oh, that we once more might wander
  As of old by Neidpath's Tower,
See again the sunset's splendour
  At the ev'ning's parting hour.

Hear the Raeburn gently singing
  Fairy songs of mystic spell ;
Happy hours such sweet thoughts bringing
  That so rare in mem'ry dwell.

Sweet the friendship, true and tender,
  Woven in the loom of life,
Heart to heart can ever render
  'Mid the never-ceasing strife.

Leave behind thee care and sadness—
  Like a canker they would eat
From thy soul all heaven-born gladness
  That makes earth so rich and sweet.

Come, then, come—of bright hours dreaming,
  On through classic scenes we'll stray,
Where a thousand charms are teeming,
  Beautifying life's short day.

'Tis the warp and woof of sorrow,
  Wild unrest, and toil, and strife,
That would steal from each glad morrow
  All the joys that sweeten life.

City life of push and glitter
  Chills the heart and dulls the brain,
Till existence, growing bitter,
  Sinks beneath in dreary pain.

From the wildwoods gaily springing
  Rise the warbling minstrels' song,
To our souls their music's bringing
  Newer life and vigour strong.

Come, then, wander by the river
  Where we've sung in happy glee ;
Watch the ripple's playing ever
  As 'tis flowing to the sea.

Thus we press our invitation,
  From the city haste away,
And in friendship's sweet elation
  Spend by Tweed thy holiday.

MARY O' ETTRICK'S GREEN GLEN.

AIR—"Jessie, the Flower o' Dumblane."

The red sun at e'en kiss'd the hill o' Pernassie,
   And the muirfowl lay hid in its ain cosy den,
When, true to the tryste wi' my ain bonnie lassie,
   I hasten'd to meet her in Ettrick's green glen.
In a' the wide warl' there is nane like sweet Mary,
   For bricht is the glance o' her bonnie dark e'e ;
Sae faultless her form, hoo she steps like a fairy—
   Oh, rich are the charms make her dear unto me.

I kenna nor carena for braw gouden treasure
   That aft brings to the heart but a sad load o' care,
Nor can it be named wi' the soul-thrillin' pleasure
   That lies in the love o' my lassie sae fair.
She's rare as the flow'ret sae stainless in blossom,
   The sharp sting o' pain maun her heart never ken ;
While joy, like a jewel, shall dwell in the bosom
   O' Mary, dear Mary in Ettrick's green glen.

Sing on thy sweet sang, thou pure, soft-flowing river ;
   Sing on, bonnie bird, owre yon bracken-clad lea :
For yonder's the lassie that I shall lo'e ever,
   Oh, sune we shall meet 'neath the auld trystin'-tree ;
When hand linked in hand, my ain darlin' Mary,
   The swift oors o' joy thegither we'll spen'—
The blythest o' a' 'neath the stars in the cairy
   Wi' thee, fairest lassie, in Ettrick's green glen.

AT THE POET'S GRAVE.*

In childhood oft the eager ears have strained
To catch the song thy humble muse had framed,
For proud were we the patriot bard to know
To whose rude harp our town so much did owe.
'Twas from thy tongue and his, the dear-lov'd sire,
First fell the words that woke song's stirring fire
And taught to love the heart-enthralling name
Of Burns, who lives, the Bard of deathless fame.

To-day we slowly tread o'er sacred ground,
And bend with reverence above the mound
Where rests in peace thy dust till God's great day,
When sounds the trump and angel voices say :
" Up, up," the Great Eternal sends the call,
The judgment's come, and doom awaiteth all.
Thus as we stand we dream of life's bright years,
Aglow with hopes that knew not cares nor fears.

Above me gleams the summer's golden sun,
Beneath the dust that life's strange race has run ;
Above there flit the birds on fleeting wing,
Below the the grass, the flowers in beauty spring.

---

* Johnny Ha', as he was familiarly known and spoken of in
Selkirk, was a worthy son of the old burgh, a stockingmaker to
trade, and, like many others, had his failings ; yet when occasion
demanded, proved himself fearless in the use of the rhymer's pen in
seeking to protect the rights of the town. He died 20th Dec.,
1872, aged 61 years. A handsome tombstone was erected to his
memory in the Old Churchyard.

How strange that each knows change, and so must we,
Our day shall quickly pass, and soon with thee,
Our cross laid down, within the tomb we'll rest,
Nor care nor grief shall e'er annoy our breast.

A BROTHER'S THOCHTS ON HIS SISTER'S WEDDIN' NICHT.

An' sae oor Nellie's gaun to leave the dear auld folk at
    hame,
To hae a haudin' o' her ain, and bear anither's name !
Fond mem'ry, dreamin', wanders owre the blythesome,
    bygone years,
An' visions o' the past arise, wi' a' their hopes an' fears.

Methinks, ance mair, within yon cot a bairnie's wail I hear,
Which tell't to aulder heids than mine a new-born babe
    was near :
What rapture then my wee heart felt when on that bairn I
    gazed—
That lassie oors, my sister, too—losh ! I was fair amaz'd.

"An' whae daur take oor bonnie bairn ?" I said wi' voice
    an' e'e ;
An' no for a' man's gouden gear that bairnie wad I gie.
She grew a sonsy, merry thing, weel lo'ed by ane an' a' ;
Her twa een shone like star-lit gems, her hair hung ringlets
    braw.

An' aft I laugh, e'en to mysel', as mem'ry, on her track,
E'en shows me forth in merry games, wi' Nellie on my
　　back :
But what cared I while, licht o' heart, I took o' play my
　　spell
Hale afternoons wi' bools or ba's wi' laddies like mysel'.

Belyve she grew an' gaed to schule ; but still she was my
　　care
When dad was oot an' mither toil'd for us baith lang an'
　　sair.
'Twas me she cam' to wi' her cares an' a' her schule-time
　　fears ;
I did my best to cheer her on an' dry her saut, saut tears.

An' noo she's grown to womanhood, an' e'en this nicht
　　she'll lea'
The dearest, kindest twa on earth (sae think their bairnies
　　three) ;
She's gaun to make anither hame—a hame that's a' her
　　ain,
She has a true man's love, an' noo a double joy she'll
　　gain.

Your brother's word, then, Nellie, take : Gin ye be leal an'
　　true
Ye needna fear but your guidman will aye be true to you.
'Tis love that soothes the weary heart an' drives away dull
　　care ;
It clears the hoose o' dreary strife, an' makes the warld
　　look fair.

Be eident aye, nor glunch, nor gloom, as ye your wark
　　maun dae ;
Juist dae it wi' a cheerfu' heart, while liltin' some bit lay ;
Ye ken, sang lichtens labour an' gies weary toilers joy,
It robs cauld care o' hauf its sting that wad ane's peace
　　destroy.

Then, take advice, dear sister mine ! juist this ae word frae
　　me :
Be true to John, an' never fear but he'll be true to thee.
Oh ! may oor Faither guard ye baith, and guide ye
　　evermair ;
An' may ye trust His love an' grace is a' your brother's
　　pray'r !

THE TOON WHERE I WAS BORN.

Though some may ca' your ancient name,
　　A charm it bears for me ;
'Twad draw me back, if I should roam
　　In lands oot owre the sea,
To tread wi' pride the dear-lo'ed streets,
　　Ne'er heedin' laughs o' scorn—
Sae dear's the spell words fail to tell,
　　Auld toon where I was born.
　　　　I canna gang, I winna gang
　　　　　Oot owre the sea at morn ;
　　　　Life's richest joys I find in thee
　　　　　The toon where I was born.

Oh, bricht the sun shines on the hames
    O' frem'd an' freen's sae dear,
An' life steps on its canny gait
    Wi' little din or steer;
Yet honest hearts are ever found
    Its annals to adorn,
Then dear's the spell nae words can tell,
    Auld toon where I was born.

E'en though the years gae fleetly by,
    An' heids grow auld an' grey,
'Twill be as dear to ilk warm heart
    As in life's brichtest day.
As seeks the bairn its mother's breast,
    Sae seeks the heart forlorn,
The lo'esome spell words canna tell,
    Auld toon where I was born.

GIN THE SHOON FITS WEAR THEM.

For senseless, menseless, silly asses
Commend me to some weel-faur'd lasses;
Where'er they be it disna matter,
Like mill wheels, tongues gang clitter-clatter.

Wi' smeddum they have ne'er been gifted
Or Clootie a' they've ha'en has lifted;
I've heard a fouth o' monkeys chatter,
But losh, *they* tongues were something sautter.

Five hunner cannon red-wud roarin',
A thoosand sleepers loodly snorin',
Forby a guid wheen hammers ringin',
Wad be as lav'rocks sweetly singin'.

I'd rather meet a stingin' ether
Than wi' sic tappies e'er forgether ;
The smiddy files gaun rispin', raspin',
Can ne'er compare wi' their mou's gaspin'.

When ance their tongues gang whitter-whatter,
Wi' noise far waur than flooded water,
Ye Po'ers abune, oh, gie them smeddum,
Else ne'er a lad will woo an' wed them.

'Tis aft declared by a' the classes
That Scotland's dow'r'd wi' braw, guid lasses ;
Gin sic's her dochter's, Scotland's sinkin',
Or else guid sense has ta'en to drinkin'.

EPISTLE TO BETTY BLETHER,
MY AULD FRIEN' AN' WORTHY NEIBOR
(A well-known local Scotch writer.)

Hech, sirs, wark's yokin's ance mair owre,
An' we hae leave 'mid Nature's dower
   To blythely wander free,
Where nane may stay the strayin' feet
As deep we drink o' ilka sweet
   On sunny hill an' lea.

Oor wealth o' gear may be but sma',
   But richer joys are oors ;
While we can watch the gloamin' **fa'**
   Amang oor ain sweet flo'ers,
      Where bloomin', perfumin'
        Ilk breath o' simmer air,
      Sae sweetly they fleetly
        Ding doon the sting o' care.

'Tis twenty years sin' first we met,
Auld freen', that time I'll ne'er forget,
   Mair youthfu' joys we knew ;
But Time rows on its flowin' stream,
An' we can mind as 'twere a dream,
   The dear-lo'ed then **sae few.**
But we are spared an' still we feel,
   Auld freen' wi' honest heart,
That we can wish each other weel—
  Nor may oor joys depart,
      But ever, for ever,
        Oor bliss increased may be ;
      Nor sadness, but gladness,
        Like gems beam in ilk e'e.

Nae doot we've mony changes seen
Sin' first the Gala met oor e'en—
   Ay, mair than tongue can tell,
Or yet can sketch wi' willin' pen,
For 'mang them a' fu' weel we ken
   Owre a' ye bear the bell.

Tho' some, wha haud life's yerkin tether,
  An' let the tongue wag free,
Say a' ye write is but a blether,
  Not worth an odd bawbee—
    Ne'er heedin', but screedin',
      Still cheer the hearts o' a'
    Wha ken yet the pen yet
      Sends sorrow to the wa'.

'Tis true that grief wi' heavy hand
Whiles bears us doon till scarce we stand,
  An' tears will drappin' fa',
But freen'ship's sympatheesin' word,
Can take the edge frae grief's sharp sword
  An' frae us turn't awa'.
Then through the breast there sune may steal
  That which makes life mair sweet,
An' ye are gifted, sae we feel,
  To make fu' rich the treat.
    That cheers us, endears us
      To Scotland's Doric tongue,
    Sae thrillin', when willin"
      'Tis blythely read or sung.

Then while ye steer alang life's way,
An' shines the sun owre hill an' brae,
  May you an' yours be bless'd ;
Nor ocht e'er seek your joys to spoil
While wi' the willin' pen ye toil,
  Nor may it ever rest.

L

For while lo'ed Ettrick sings its sang,
 An' Tweed an' Gala meet,
Or rustic rhymes still clink fu' thrang,
 An' we can ither greet.
  Sae cheerie, nor weary,
   A freen' I'll claim thee mine,
  An' blythely, an' kythely,
   Ye weel may ca' me thine.

THE LAND I LOVE.

I love thee well, my native land,
 Thou'rt rugged, grand, and free ;
Each bosky dell, each craggy steep,
 Each verdant, flow'ry lea
Awake emotions in my breast
 That ever proudly swell,
No other land on all the earth
 Can I e'er love so well.

Hail, land ! thou home of beauty bright,
 What sense and worth are thine,
That trample down the might of wrong,
 While truths triumphant shine.
Eternal as the voice of God
 Our freedom aye shall reign,
Free as the air our spirits breathe,
 Our souls shall bear no chain.

Hail, land ! where in the darken'd past,
  Upon thy green hill-sides,
Arose the holy psalm and pray'r,
  And flow'd in crimson tides
The blood of those who lov'd their God,
  Nor would to tyrants give
The guidance of their souls' true faith
  In Him through Whom we live.

Oft, oft I've stood in boyhood's years
  Where steel rang sharp on steel,
And " right " and "might " together met—
  Oh, who to earth would reel.
Methought I saw their forces meet *
  Where good Sir David led,
Along the Linglie heath-crowned heights
  And fast by Ettrick's bed.

Lo ! Yarrow thou art reached at last,
  Where sounds of battle rung,
Where faithful Leslie hotly press'd,
  And from the godless tongue
The dark oaths fell ; ah ! who can tell
  The feelings of each soul,
While stroke on stroke is sharply struck
  And foemen earthwards roll.

---

  * The battle of Philiphaugh was fought on the 13th September, 1645—the Royalists being led by the Marquis of Montrose, and the Covenanters by Sir David Leslie.

My native town, what hopes, what fears
   Thou centred there that day,
The Souter's awl lay idle then
   That each might watch and pray.
" Say ! who shall win ? Pray God, the right,"
   Each one in heart hath said.
Hurrah ! 'tis done ; o'er Minchmuir fast
   The proud Montrose hath fled.

And, lo ! there breaks upon my ears
   From out that darken'd time,
Up-welling from those hearts so brave,
   A psalm of thanks sublime.
The God of battles strength He gave
   To stem usurping might ;
All fearless of the godless hosts,
   They fought for " God and right."

My native land, I love thee well,
   And hope still brighter grows
Within my breast, a day shall dawn
   When, free from wrong's dark woes,
To Him who hath our country bless'd
   There shall with joy arise
One song of praise that ever more
   Shall echo through the skies.

As shines yon sun resplendent now
   O'er fields of golden grain,
So sure shall tears of sorrow cease
   And pangs of bitter pain ;

When patriot hearts so firm and true
　Shall toil with willing hand
All wrong to slay, and bless with joy
　My own loved native land.

TO A BEAUTIFUL CHILD.

　　　" Come to me, child,"
Rich gift from the Omniscient Divine,
Let me look on that sweet face of thine,
And gaze deep down into those star-lit eyes
Aglow with life—God-life that never dies.
For lov'd one thou art pure without, within,
All stainless of the loathsome marks of sin ;
Nor angels robed in all their splendour bright,
Amid the glory of eternal light,
Outvie that soul of thine, sweet babe so fair,
With clear, bright azure eyes and nut-brown hair.
But coming years, borne on the stream of Time,
With changing moods, soft as a Runic rhyme,
What will they bring to thee, thou lovely child,
Thou image rare of the Undefiled ?
Griefs, heart-torture, too deep for bitter tears,
Pain, that ever the soul with sadness sears.
Or sunk in sin, scorn'd and pass'd on the street
Like horrid filth we tread beneath our feet.

Oh, pure, sweet child !
The loving soul revolts to dream of this,
Nay, it must not be, thou art an heir of bliss ;
And yet as I gaze into that young face,
And each line of beauty lovingly trace,
The truth wells up of the pure ones born
Who have died the death of despair and scorn.
Though ever across from the heavenly shore,
Where open wide stands Mercy's door,
Came the voice of Love bidding wand'rers come
From the paths afar to their soul's own home,
Yet, alas ! they died such a death of shame,
Shrieking, groaning, cursing God's holy name.

Beautiful child !
Angel of peace and heaven-sent gem of bliss,
Thy rosebud lips breathe words ears would not miss,
And thy rippling laugh in its richest tone
Is music sweet the angel bands might own.
What thou wilt be is hid from earth-born eyes
Like the glory that lies beyond the skies ;
To Him who knoweth all we bow and pray —
Do Thou step by step over life's strange way
Lead by the hand, full of meekness mild,
Past temptations strong, this Thine own child.
A bringer of gladness and heart-thrilling bliss,
A sweetner of woe with love's holy kiss,
Sunshine, 'mid sadness where'er thou may'st be—
Such is the future we pray for thee.

OOR AULD HAME.

Oh ! oor auld hame, oor auld hame,
    That rang wi' mirth an' glee,
When in the bygane years we ran,
    Three merry bairnies wee ;
But changes hae come owre us a'—
    Ilk ane their gait has gane,
And sae we meet nae as we met
    Aroond the auld hearthstane.

Oh ! oor auld hame, oor auld hame,
    What mem'ries ye reca'
O' gentle words and lovin' smiles,
    And scenes noo pass'd awa'.
They're twin'd aroond oor hearts, **nor** shall
    The sweetness frae them wane ;
Oh ! gin we were but bairnies yet
    Aroond the auld hearthstane.

Oh ! oor auld hame, oor auld hame,
    That's tasted joy and wae,
This nicht it rings wi' bridal mirth,
    That gars ilk heart feel gay ;
The youngest o' us a' has got
    A guidman o' her ain :
And brichtly may the lowe o' love
    Burn on their ain hearthstane.

Oh ! oor auld hame, oor auld hame
   We ne'er will cease to lo'e ;
Though we may wander far awa',
   Oor hearts will aye be true.
May blessin's richer than we've seen
   Be thine, unmix'd wi' pain,
And lang may He who dwells aboon
   Reign owre the auld hearthstane.

THE HOME OF THE FREE.

AIR—" Oh Erin, my country."

Old Scotland, dear homeland, thy hills and thy dales.
Are shrines of sweet songs and heart-thrilling tales,
Thy mountains uprearing in beauty I see,
Thy lakes silver gleam by the homes of the free,
   Thy grandeur enthralls me, I love only thee—
   Scotland, brave Scotland, the home of the free !

To wander away o'er the blue ocean's breast,
And seek for a home 'mid the lands of the West :
My heart would but fail me, I love only thee,
Thou beautiful island, strong girt by the sea.

Enchained by the spirit of freedom, that dwells
On thy green mountain sides and thy flow'r-spangled dells,
Like thy rivers deep-flooded, so love flows for thee,
Proud land of the thistle, the brave and the free.

IN THE STRAND.

Chiming bells of St Clement Danes
Softly pealing mysterious strains.
Love's tender song 'tis sweet to me,
Life and joy in its melody ;
Heart throbbings passionate and strong,
Casting spells o'er the restless throng ;
Bringing in dreams—vale and hill,
The blackbirds song, the tinkling rill ;
Bringing to mem'ry, oh ! so fair,
Forms of beauty matchless there.

Chiming bells of St Clement Danes,
Pealing out o'er earth's weary pains,
Clear silver tones fall on the ears,
Out of thy clanging brightness and tears ;
In dreams there roam o'er moor and vale
Youth and maid whisp'ring low love's tale,
Heedless of day's swift winging flight ;
Careless while fall the shades of night,
Bending low 'tis thus whispers he—
　"She is a' the world to me,
　　And for bonnie Annie Laurie
　I would lay me doon and dee."

Thrilling bells of St Clement Danes,
Chiming at mid-day love's sweet strains ;
Stealing o'er the din of the Strand,
Stealing the heart in love's fair band.
Years in their flight have come and gone,

Yet fancy hears each familiar tone
Rising, falling, trilling so free—
    "She is a' the world to me."
Heart be true as those tender strains,
Rung so rich from St Clement Danes.

ADDRESS TO FANCY.

ON THE AFRICAN EXPLORATION EXPEDITION.

(The terrible accounts given in the public press of the doings of
what is known as the " Stanley Rear Column " must have stirred
within the breasts of many feelings of indignation that anyone pro-
fessing to be a British subject could have any connection with such
barbarism.)

Hail, Fancy, lo'ed an' life-lang freen',
Wha draws for me on Dream's fair screen
    Wi' deft, unerring hand
The matchless grace o' beauty rare,
Or heart-sad scenes o' waefu' care
    That owre aft stain oor land,
Didst bring across the briny deep,
    Frae Afric's forests dark,
Sad tales that move the strang to weep
    An' 'neath love's lowest mark.
      'Tis sad'nin', an' mad'nin',
        The cruel deeds o' shame
      That's wingin' an' ringin'
        Against oor British name.

Wha bears a heart God made to feel
The richt or wrang o' human weal,
  But beats wi' indignatien
To ken that murder's gleamin' knife,
Or but the bitter cords o' strife,
  Hae cursed a lowly nation.
A little maid, some mither's pride—
  Oh, God, can this be true ?
That frae her heart flow'd life's red tide
  (Was he insane who knew ?)
      They socht her an' bocht her
        That cruel death to die,
     Nor mov'd he nor prov'd he
        A Briton brave was nigh.

Dark demon deeds, infinite scorn
Within ilk honest breast be born
  'Gainst a' wha woman harm,
Or raise the cruel lash on high,
Nor spare though victims sink an' die,
  While flows the life-blood warm.
Oh, graceless wretch ! to kick the bairn.
  Had he nae laddie days ?
Or had his heart become like airn
  As he wee Soudy slays ?
      Inhuman, wha slew man,
        The beings God gave breath ;
     Unfeelin', revealin'
        He weel deserved his death.

Hoo can they trust the white man's God ·
They're taught as bearin' life's vast load
   An' blessin' ane an' a'?
Sic fiendish monsters free o' love
To Afric's tribes maun surely prove
   Oor God's nae God ava.
Sae reason thus may bid them think,
   While girn and curse maun steer
Their darken'd thochts near ruin's brink
   Through hatefu', abject fear.
      Oh, madness an' sadness
        That wrings the human breast,
      To flight man frae white man
        They canna but detest.

Yet, Fancy, say can such be true,
'Twad maist make Britons sadly rue
   They bear a Briton's name ;
The indignation hearts maun speak
Will mantle on ilk manly cheek
   The deep-dyed blush o' shame.
A Briton brave—an insane fool
   Ilk ane maun surely been
Wha gazed on sic dark deeds o' dool,
   Nor prov'd the wrang'd ane's freen'.
      Sae shame, then, nor fame, then,
        Be theirs through lastin' time
      Wha aided, nor stay'd it,
        Wild murder's horrid crime.

Oor glorious flag an' Bible grand
We seek to plant on every land
   Where shines the gouden sun ;
But freedom nor salvation's plan
Shall ever win the heart o' man
   While deeds like these are done.
'Tis gentleness o' love alane
   The heart an' soul that thrills
To leave the gods o' wud an' stane
   An' bow to Him wha fills
      Supernal, eternal,
        Wi' love the warld fair,
        Though madness an' sadness
        Aft sear the soul wi' care.

To Him, the God o' earth an' sea,
At His ain throne we bow the knee,
   An' thus we humbly pray :
Do Thou in Thy great po'er divine
(For Thou hast said, " Vengeance is mine,")
   Sic deeds guid Lord repay ;
Yet Thou ken'st best what should be dune
   In a' that's guid or ill.
Guid Lord, we pray, lead a' abune
   To blend wi' Thine their will—
      Believin', receivin'
        The strength to shun a crime ;
       An' rivin', an' strivin'
        Earth we shall make sublime.

THE LASSIE WHA'S RAREST O' A'.

Oh ken ye wee Annie, she's blythe an' she's cannie,
  O' Gala's fair lassies she's rarest o' a' ;
Sae gladly I'll meet her an' lovingly greet her
  Far doon in the dell where the sweet blue-bells blaw.
She's lithesome an' cheerie, nane wi' her can weary
  An' love like a jewel gleams bricht in her e'e,
When comes the grey gloamin' wi' her I'll gae roamin',
  The sweet words to win that shall bind her to me.

Oh wha could be cruel to sic a rare jewel,
  Or yet cause the tears owre her saft cheeks to fa',
The snawdraps white bosom though pure be its blossom
  Can match nae wi' Annie, the fairest o' a'.
The heart's fondly beatin' wi' dreams o' oor meetin'
  Dear lassie wha's voice is rich music to me ;
Oh hasten thou gloamin', for then I'll gae roamin'
  Through Elwand's fair dell when the stars glint on hie.

AMANG THE BAIRNS.

AIR—"The Lea Rig."

———

The e'enin' brings the bairns a' hame,
   Ilk ane their tale to tell, guidman,
Hoo they hae wander'd a' the day
   Through wud an' flo'ery dell, guidman.
There's Jamie wi' the lauchin' een,
   An' Bell, oor pawkie dearie, O,
An' Jock, an' Tam, an' noisy Rab,
   The hoose they haud fu' cheerie, O.

There's Jock play'd truant frae the schule
   To gang an' pu' the slaes, guidman ;
By Jenny Sharp's, losh, Tam gaed oot
   To speel the whinny braes, guidman.
When Buckholm Hill was set alowe,
   I maist fell tapsalteerie, O,
When tauld that twa o' oors were there,
   Their hame-come made me weary, O.

An' where the Gala wimples roond
   The Rye-haugh braw an' green, guidman,
'Tis whisper'd Bell an' twa-three mair
   Like flo'er-clad queens were seen, guidman.
An' where the Bakehouse burn rins clear
   Owre aft wades ilka dearie, O.
But e'enin' brings the bairns a' hame,
   Where love lets nane grow weary, O.

The e'enin' brings the bairns a' hame,
   Where ilka ane finds rest, guidman ;
When there they tell owre a' their ploys
   Upon their mother's breast, guidman.
An' when life's e'enin' comes to a'
   As cam' ilk youthfu' dearie, O,
May a' airt Hame to joys that last,
   Where dule nor care comes near ye, O.

SAVED AT LAST.

(WITH SONG.)

PERSONAGES REPRESENTED—THE DRUNKARD AND HIS SISTER.

THE DRUNKARD'S SOLILOQUY.

Is it true that here I wander,
   Like the winds that round me blow,
Floating with life's flowing river,
   Careless how or where I go ?
Wand'ring ever, staying never,
   Dreaming dreams of fancy bright ;
Or in madness wildly rushing
   'Mid the hateful scenes of night.

Ever drifting—onward drifting,
   Like a helpless ship at sea ;
Without one ray of hope to brighten
   Cheerless life on earth to me.

Like a slave, I feel around me
   Clasp'd a bitter galling chain;
And my breast is ever burning,
   With a horrid craving pain.
Never sleeping, it is crying,
   Give me drink, Oh, give me drink ;
Like a slave, by blood-hounds hunted,
   Shall I like their victim sink ?

Yes, 'tis true, I well remember
   That like jewels, sparkling bright,
Was the tiny glass I handled
   On that merry marriage night.
Never saw I so much beauty
   As my eyes look'd round on there,
For it seem'd to me each maiden
   Was an angel pure and fair ;
As they through the dance soft glided.
   Swift the night hours pass'd along,
While our ears enchanted listen'd
   To their voices sweet in song.

Yes, 'tis true, thou'st felt the power
   Of sweet love's enthralling spell ;
Winning smiles, and sweet words spoken,
   And thy heaven was turn'd to hell.

The jewell'd hand of blushing bridesmaid
   Gave the bright, the brimming cup,
And with smiles to me the rarest,
   Bade me quaff the rich wine up.

M

Oh, the horror ! yes, I drank it,
　　Till my soul was in a flame,
And to-night I stand a drunkard,
　　Lost in misery and in shame.
Love of kindred, God, and country
　　From my heart by drink are torn ;
With the pangs of anguish gnawing,
　　Down life's current I am borne.

And it seems the night winds blowing
　　Bear along those fiendish eyes,
That are ever at me leering,
　　Whilst this inward craving cries
With a cry that's never ceasing,
　　Which I cannot, cannot still,
Though it fills my soul with loathing
　　And destroys my power of will.
Were it mine that land call'd Heaven,
　　I'd exchange it for strong drink,
Though it drags me ever downwards
　　O'er the verge of ruin's brink.

Back, ye fiends, around me pressing,
　　Back, and leave my brain alone ;
Back to your home, yon dark abyss—
　　Oh, my God ! they'll not begone !

Bring to me the crystal goblet
　　Fill'd with nectar most divine ;
And be truce to care and sadness,
　　Let us drown them deep in wine.

Oh, the madness of this craving
   That within is ever mine;
I must drink though I should perish—
   Bring me wine, one cup of wine.

THE SISTER'S SONG.

AIR—" The Gipsy's Warning."

Do not touch the wine cup, brother,
   Of its deadly spell beware,
It will fill thy heart with sorrow,
   Sink thy soul in dark despair.
Yes, 'twill rob thee of life's brightness,
   Shunn'd by all thou soon wouldst be;
Listen to thy sister's pleading,
   From the wine cup, oh, be free.

Do not touch the wine cup, brother,
   Leave, ah, leave its haunts, and come
Where in freedom sweetly smiling
   We in joy can ever roam.
There thy heart will lose its sadness,
   Life to thee will nobler be;
Listen to thy sister's pleading,
   From the wine cup's pow'r be free.

Do not touch the wine cup, brother,
   Once our home knew nought of care;
But dark clouds of sorrow low'ring,
   Throw their blighting shadows there.

Pledge thyself with manly courage,
 Friends will help and cherish thee ;
Listen to thy sister's pleading,
 From the wine cup now be free.

THE DRUNKARD'S REPLY.

Thanks to God ! love's gentle pleading
 Bids me strive once more to be
Strong to fight in life's rough battle,
 From the drink curse ever free.
And I pledge me, Heaven aiding,
 That, however hard the fight,
I shall dare, through all temptation,
 God to serve and do the right ;
And to tell, while on life's journey,
 This sad story of the past,
And rejoice, a sister's pleading
 Has the drunkard saved at last.

CHILDHOOD'S DAYS.

INSCRIBED TO THE PLORA LODGE, I.O.G.T., WALKERBURN.

AIR—" Memories Dear."

Hoo rich are life's joys in the bricht days o' childhood,
 Sae lichtsome the heart that it kens nae o' care ;
The hours fleet awa' like a calm flowin' river,
 Sweet scented wi' flo'ers o' simmer sae fair.

An' sic castles are built, although they maun crumble,
   Their buildin', indeed, to the bairnies brings glee ;
An', oh ! hoo they dream o' the year's joyous endin'
   That aye brings alang wi't a rare Christmas tree.
         Oh ! childhood's days.

Hoo hearty an' grand are the dear games o' childhood,
   Their laughter rings lood ower the hill an' the glen ;
Ower their lessons unlearn'd the mithers are flytin',
   While bairnies plead sair they ne'er thocht it was ten.
Sae late in the gloamin' by the fireside sittin',
   Their dreams seem to brichten the licht in ilk e'e ;
Oh, what can it be ! 'Tis the year's joyous endin'
   That aye brings alang wi't a rare Christmas tree.
         Oh ! childhood's days.

God bless the dear bairnies, an' may they be ever
   Led by His ain hand owre the pathway o' life ;
An' may a' their joys be as pure as their childhood's,
   Unstain'd by the wae o' the drunkard's sad strife.
An' when in life's e'enin' o' childhood they're dreamin',
   Though nearin' the gates o' the bricht land on hie,
They'll tell hoo they lang'd for the year's joyous endin'
   That aye brocht alang wi't a rare Christmas tree.
         Oh ! childhood's days.

A CRACK OWRE DRINK.

(ACCEPT O'T WHA MAY.)

" O' a' the ills poor Caledonia
    E'er yet pree'd, or e'er will taste,
  Brewed in hell's black Pandemonia,
    Whisky's ill will scaith her maist ! '
                —H. MACNEIL.

Drink oot yer dram, what need we care
  Ilk godly saunt's objections,
Or a' the whee-geein' o' oor freends
  An' their profess'd affections.
Drink aff your dram, this life is oors
  To fill wi' grief or pleasure ;
Then droon cauld care an' heeze up mirth
  In ae guid lucky measure.

Hoot, toots ! it sets the tongue agaun
  In ilka social gath'rin' ;
Ne'er fash your thoom though gossips think
  That a' your talk's but bleth'rin' ;
Wi' social mirth in crack or sang
  It sets man's tongue a-bummin',
An' oh ! the glorious po'er it wields
  Owre peerless, dear-lo'ed woman.

The prim mou', hech ! drink sets aside,
  The e'e hoo bricht it glitters ;
The thocht sublime, or clootie slang,
  Wakes her to wanton titters.

What need we heed though foreign loons
   Ca' oors a drucken nation ;
Or though, to please oor self-conceit,
   We lose oor soul's Salvation,

But steek your heart 'gainst selfish pride,
   The same 'gainst sinfu' folly ;
An' oh ! be wise, nor let your soul
   Sink low wi' melancholy.
Though true it is this life's a fecht,
   An' roond us there lies danger,
May joy an' fun, twin sisters guid,
   Ne'er think your heart a stranger.

Owre true the demon ca'd Despair
   Has made some stop an' swither,
Gin they wad still trudge life's gait owre
   Or end it a' thegither.
But na ! Across their tortur'd brain
   Grim thochts o' fear come jinkin',
An' sae to droon the sad pest, Care,
   They start e'en to the drinkin'.

Frae Clootie's den some fiendish imp
   (The thocht was never human)
Whisper'd " strang drink can fill the soul
   O' either man or woman ; "
But could we hear the waefu' mane
   That through that den is ringin',
I dootna but the leevin' here
   Glad changes sune wad bring in.

But draw Death's curtain to a side
 An' lost anes frae ilk station,
Wi' mad'nin' mane will fill your ears
 That drink's distill'd damnation ;
That heaven's robb'd, an' hell is fill'd,
 Though God's ain sel' is pleadin'
Frae evil to abstain an' seek
 His grace ilk ane is needin'.

Drink aff your dram, the nicht wears late
 An' winter winds are blawin' ;
Drink aff your dram, starvation times
 Are closely round us drawin' ;
An' bairns an' wives may greet an' grane
 For guid meat an' for cleedin',
Oor noble sel's let's pledge again,
 Guid-nicht, for time is speedin'.

SAVE OUR LAND.

Air—" Rolling Home."

Land of freedom oft we hail thee,
 Home of all that's true and grand ;
Oft we sing there is no country
 Like to thee our native land.

But though tyrants ne'er oppress us,
  Till the drink-curse cease to be
There's a stain upon thy banner,
  Glorious island of the sea.

> Save our land, save our land,
>   Save our land from drink's dark stain,
> Ye who love a life of freedom
>   Break the drunkard's galling chain.

Oft we praise thy hills and valleys,
  And thy streamlets winding clear,
Every flower that blooms upon thee
  To the patriot heart is dear.
But the shame and heartfelt sorrow
  Many thousands feel in thee,
Bids us toil, nor failing ever
  Till our land from drink is free.
    Save our land, &c.

See our noble standard waving
  Like a beacon star of light,
In the vanguard forward pressing,
  Let us never fear the fight.
Freedom from the drunkard's evils
  Ever must our watchword be,
Patriot deeds must cleanse thy banner,
  Glorious island of the sea,
    Save our land, &c.

A SONG OF HOPE.

We'll make the years far better yet
    Than ever they hae been,
For love an' joy will brichtly burn
    To glad this earth's fair scene.
Though wi' its sting strong drink has cursed
    An' darken'd earth wi' care,
'Tis oors to bring it a' aboot—
    Earth made like snowdrops fair.

We'll make the years far better yet,
    We'll wipe the fa'in tears,
An' hearts far sunk 'neath sorrow's cluds
    We'll free them o' a' fears.
The world will ring wi' jocund sang ;
    On earth we want nae mair
Than hearts wi' truth made bauld an' free,
    Like snowdrops pure an' fair.

We'll make the years far better yet—
    The dowie bits o' weans
Wha wear the drunkard's bairnie's claes
    An' dree its waesome pains ;
Like Ane Wha bade them come to Him,
    Let's cheer the heart that's sair,
An' make them what they aye should be—
    Like snowdrops pure an' fair.

We'll make the years far better yet—
    We'll closer band this nicht
To bear the Templar standard on
    In true Guid Templar micht ;
For Scottish hearts can never fail
    When they but manfu' dare
To slay a wrang, an' make their land
    To bloom like snowdrops fair.

We'll make the years far better yet,
    For doon the vale o' Time
We'll ring the glorious "guidwill" sang
    In tones love makes sublime ;
An' gouden gates will lifted be
    For grand's the welcome there
To drink's slaves free, wha'll ever be
    Like snowdrops pure an' fair.

WHAT ABOOT THE BAIRNS?

An' what aboot the bairns, puir things ?
    Is there nane to care ava
For the dowie look o' ilk wee face
    An' the heavy tear-drap's fa' ?
Is there nane to heed their cry for breid,
    Save wi' a cruel straik ?
There's room for a' to fecht 'gainst drink,
    That gars the wee hearts ache.

An' what aboot the bairns, puir things,
   Hauf-cled wi' tatter'd claes ?
When winds seuch lood oot owre the land,
   They nip their bits o' taes.
An' wild some race an' rin aboot,
   Dark aiths frae their lips fa',
Learn'd aft at hame through waefu' drink,
   That brings sair grief to a'.

An' what aboot the bairns, puir things,
   God's gifts to you an' me ?
Maun souls, bricht gems that are His ain,
   Sink doon in sin an' dee ?
Oh, cowards a' wha sit an' sneer,
   An' cry that's nocht o' mine ;
" Am I my brither's keeper?"   " Yes,"
   Is God's ain word divine.

An' what aboot the bairns, puir things ?
   Their wail maun heav'nwards ring,
Till ane an' a' shall manfu' act,
   An' drink's po'er doonwards fling.
God gie us strength to work for Him,
   An' for the bairns, puir things,
That joyous bliss their lives may fill,
   While praise frae ilk heart springs.

THE DRUNKARD'S WEE WEAN.

AIR—" Afton Water."

'Tis winter again, 'tis the fa' o' the year,
An' shrill its cauld blasts thro' the glens greet the ear;
The hills clad wi' bracken, the gowany lea,
Hae tint a' their beauty 'mid snaw-wreaths sae hie.

Hoo waefu' the wail o' the drunkard's wee wean,
As ill-clad he rins 'mang the snaw or the rain ;
He kens nae o' love, for there's nane seems to care
For the blink o' his e'e an' his bonnie broon hair.

Sae wistfu' he keeks through the hauf-open door,
Where oor mither sae kind minds her weans frae her store ;
An', oh ! but it's sair when ye ken that the wean
Can dream o' nae pleasures in life he has ha'en.

The drunkard's wee wean drees the warld's cauld froon',
Sair, sair in his rags the wee wean's hauden doon ;
Ne'er wonder that tears dim the licht o' his e'e,
Nor beats his young heart wi' the brichtness o' glee.

His hame, like the winter, is cauldness itsel',
When blythe bleezed the ingle there's nae ane can tell.
Sae dreary an' dark is the look o' the room,
Wha'd blame him for fearin' to bide in its gloom ?

The drunkard's wee wean, oh, wha wadna strive
To save frae the fate that to ruin may drive,
An' tell him o' Ane wha a Faither will prove,
An' shelter his soul wi' the richest o' love.

TRUE BRITONS. (?)

(Suggested on hearing " Rule Britannia " sung in a public-house.)

"No, Britons never shall be slaves,"
　　Hark to the boastful chorus,
'Tis sung with all man's pow'r of voice,
　　Behind us and before us.
They'll ne'er be slaves, and yet each coin
　　That can one drop still buy them
Too hot becomes for purse or pouch,
　　To cool it they must try them.

"Thee haughty tyrants ne'er shall tame,"
　　Hark to their cheers like thunder,
While half-starv'd children cry for bread,
　　And wives sit sad and wonder—
Why are their absent ones so late ?
　　Could they but hear them singing,
Would they feel proud to hear them thus ?
　　While drink's sad ruin bringing.

Oh, how they worship freedom's flag,
　　And danger, how they'd brave it ;
Its fair folds not a foe shall stain,
　　Their lives they'd give to save it.
A brimming bumper to our homes,
　　And loved ones there, God bless them ;
With loud hurrahs 'tis drunk by fools
　　Who'd rather kick than kiss them.

Ignoble deeds these patriots scorn,
    Detesting wrong's harsh doer ;
For " Right " each Briton nobly stands,
    Than they none can be truer.
Who sets his foot on British soil
    Shall know no claims of slav'ry ;
Then home they stagger, there to act
    With curse and blow their brav'ry.

Then once again with health and song
    They praise our war-ships sailing,
And every tar that's firm as oak,
    Though war's wild storms are railing.
Still louder yet their songs shall ring
    Of Nelson or " wight Wallace,"
Till mad with drink dark deeds they dare,
    May bring them to the gallows.

" Long live Victoria," thus they shout,
    To reign o'er our dominions ;
Long live each statesman who gives heed
    To our expressed opinions.
A bumper fill, we'll pledge it thus,
    Britannia rules the waves ;
May freedom's star still shine on us,
    Who never shall be slaves.

Oh, hollow mockery thus to sing
    Like silly fools mad raving,
While hearts and homes are wreck'd and curs'd
    And thousands bread are craving.

Awake, stand in the light of God,
  What glorious joys thou'rt missing ;
Know Britain's name for drink's become
  A bye-word and a hissing.

How glorious would our country be
  If freed from drink's cursed slav'ry,
If cast the fatal cup away,
  Unknown its fatal knav'ry.
Oh, Britons brave, breathe Freedom's air,
  In actions true, revealing
That strength from God is freely giv'n
  While you in pray'r are kneeling.

LOVE DIVINE, BEYOND DEGREE.

AIR—" Depths of Mercy."

Oh, sing the song of boundless love,
  And tell the wondrous story,
How Jesus left His throne above,
  And angel songs in glory.
Oh ! love divine, beyond degree,
To leave His throne in heaven for me !
      For me ! for me !
      He left His throne for me.

No princely halls, no queenly hands
   Received the heavenly stranger ;
His only robes were swaddling bands,
   His lowly bed a manger.
Oh, love divine, to think that He
Became an earth-born babe for me !
      For me ! for me !
      Became a babe for me.

No home had He while here on earth ;
   His path was dark and dreary.
A man of sorrows from His birth ;
   In griefs and labours weary.
Oh ! love divine, beyond degree,
To bear these sorrows all for me !
      For me ! for me !
      He bore them all for me.

Behold Him nailed to yonder tree,
   While sinners mocked around Him :
He shed His precious blood for me ;
   My sins the nails that bound Him.
Oh ! love divine, to think that He
Should bleed, and groan, and die for me !
      For me ! for me !
      He died—He died for me.

N

YET THERE'S ROOM.

Air—" At the cross there's room."

Art thou weary of thy sin ?
  At the cross there's room ;
If thou wouldst be pure within,
  At the cross there's room.
Jesus died, dear one, for thee,
Bore the shame of Calvary's tree,
That thou mightst from sin be free—
  At the cross there's room.

Pleasures fade and pass away,
  At the cross there's room ;
Jesus' love will ne'er decay,
  At the cross there's room.
Truths to light the darken'd mind,
Healing for the sick and blind,
All we need in Him we find,
  At the cross there's room.

Linger not though tempest-toss'd,
  At the cross there's room ;
Linger not, thou mightst be lost,
  At the cross there's room.
Look from self, there's nothing there ;
Look to Christ, His glory share ;
He can save from sin and care—
  At the cross there's room.

Time is passing, death is near,
  At the cross there's room ;
Jesus calls, doubt not nor fear,
At the cross there's room.
Angels whisper, come away,
All thy cares on Jesus lay,
Life Eternal have to-day—
  At the cross there's room.

LEAD THOU ME.

Weary of the world's sinning,
Weary of its bitter strife,
Jesu Saviour, Son of God,
Lead me to the higher life—
  Lead, oh ! lead Thou me.

Tired with the tempest's raging,
Tired and so fain to rest,
Jesu Saviour, Son of God,
Draw me nearer to Thy breast—
  Draw, oh ! draw Thou me.

Gladden'd by Thy Spirit's favour,
Gladden'd by Thy love so free,
Jesu Saviour, Son of God,
Life alone I find in Thee—
  Keep, oh ! keep Thou me.

THERE'S JOY BEYOND IT ALL.

AIR—"The Veteran."

I once was far from God,
   And wander'd deep in sin,
And though I tasted world's joys,
   I knew not peace within.
Yet deeper still I sank
   In Satan's hateful thrall,
Till Jesus came and woke my heart
   . To joys beyond it all.

I heard His gentle voice,
   In love it spoke to me,
And in the blood on Calvary shed
   I am from sin set free.
I know no friend like Him,
   'Tis bliss to hear His call,
And wake the heart from earthly things
   To joys beyond it all.

God's love shall draw me on
   To tread the Heavenly way
That lead's from dark temptation's pow'r
   To bright eternal day ;
But here I'll fight 'gainst sin
   Till sweet the voice shall fall
That stills my heart and calls me home
   To joys beyond it all.

TWA MEN.

Up the street there were twa men gaed,
　An' ane was fu' prood an' hie ;
He steppit oot wi' stately gait,
　Thinkin' nane sae guid could be.
Slee he lookit to see gin fouk
　Were shawin' respect to him.
Nae thocht had he that Ane would m'urn
　That his soul wi' sin grew dim.

The ither coo'r'd his heid wi' shame,
　An' heart-wailed—" Guid Lord o' a',
Dinna let's perish in my sins ;
　In thy sicht fu' low's my fa'.
I'm naething, Lord, but Ane has dee'd ;
　For His sake dae Thou forgi'e."
While he grat an' pray'd his heart grew licht,
　For sin forgi'en was he.

THE WIDOW'S MITE.

The widow's mite was mair to God
   Than the rich man's siller croon ;
The Maister ken'd in pride they gied,
   Bnt the widow's heart was soun'.

He ca'd the twal' to Him, an' said—
   " The puir body's cast in mair
Than a' the lave, weel though they've gi'en,
   For they had an' weel could spare.

" But she, rare gift fu' rich an' sweet,
   To God she's gi'en her a' ;"
Nae doot when frae His hoose she turned,
   Weel blessed she gaed awa'.

An' what to Him freens hae we gi'en ?
   Let's search oor hearts an' ken,
For noo's the time God's love to test
   Ere comes to us life's en'.

HARK! THE VOICE OF JESUS.

Weak and erring fellow-mortal,
  Sailing o'er life's sea,
In what haven will you anchor
  Through eternity.
    Hark! the voice of Jesus;
      Hark! He bids thee come;
    In His blood for all there's cleansing—
      He will save and lead thee home.

Tossing to and fro, nor dreaming
  Of the woes that fall
On those souls that slight God's warning,
  And the gospel call.

Weary soul, no longer wander
  Far from God and rest,
Long has Jesus gently pleaded
  He might be thy guest.

Sinner, ere the night has fallen
  O'er our sin-stained earth,
Let the news be borne to heaven
  Of thy soul's new birth.

FATHER, LEAD ME.

In the love of Christ I glory,
　　All things else before it fade,
'Tis a grand, a wondrous story
　　How my debt to God was paid.
　　　　Father, lead me, ever lead me
　　　　In the way that Thou wilt need me;
　　　　Father, lead me, kindly lead me
　　　　And my soul shall Thee obey.

Not with gold nor earthly treasure
　　Jesus satisfied my God,
But through love we cannot measure
　　He Himself bore sin's dark load.

Fill'd with joy, I now adore Him,
　　Blessed peace He gives to me,
And my all I lay before Him —
　　Only His I seek to be.

By Thy Spirit lead me ever
　　Faithful here to fight 'gainst sin,
Then I know beyond the river
　　" Welcome home " from Thee I'll win.

THE BIRTH OF CHRIST.

He comes, He comes, the promised One by prophets long
    foretold,
He comes to be the Living Way heaven's portals to unfold ;
But not in all the pomp of wealth the Prince of Peace
    appears,
His birth-place was no palace great, His welcome not man's
    cheers.

The Christ-babe in a stable born, low in a manger lay,
Yet angel hosts His advent sang ere woke the dawning day.
No crown press'd on His infant brow with costly diadem,
But in the sky above there shone " the Star of Bethlehem."

Go hide your heads ye proud of earth in sorrow and in
    shame,
With contrite hearts go humbly think how Christ the
    Saviour came :
God's only Son, an earth-babe born, the sinner's friend
    to be,
To burst the bonds, and help the soul to know God's liberty.

How must those shepherds' hearts have thrilled when 'mid
    the calm of night
The white robed hosts burst on their gaze halo'd in heavenly
    light,
And heard rung out in words sublime the tidings of His
    birth—
Hail, glorious song, that filled their souls, " Peace and
    goodwill to earth."

In faith they heard the wondrous strain and worship'd at
    His shrine,
Nor doubted He was Jesu, Lord, the promised Christ
    divine.
How strange to think the Son of God was thus so lowly
    born—
Go think of it who pamper self and humble birth would
    scorn.

Jesus, the son of God Triune, in lowly guise appears
To bear our sorrows and our griefs and shed for us His
    tears.
Oh ! Love Divine, beyond our power to fully realise,
May we, our wills, our all, in Thee to full fruition rise.

All hail the Christ, Immanuel, His glories loud proclaim
Till o'er the earth each soul with joy shall praise and bless
    His name ;
And lowly bending at His feet, His love by faith adorn,
To fill the earth with love and peace Jesus, the Christ,
    was born.

CHRIST THE FRIEND WE NEED.

Air—"Beautiful Words of Life."

While we're treading life's pathway here
　　Christ is the Friend we need,
Ever with joy our souls to cheer,
　　Christ is the Friend we need.
　　He can lead us onward
　　Singing happy homeward—
Wonderful Friend, Merciful Friend, Glorious Friend of all.

Sinner drifting in sin and care,
　　Christ is the Friend we need,
He alone can make life all fair,
　　Christ is the Friend we need.
　　With His blood He bought us,
　　Pleading He has sought us—
Wonderful Friend, Merciful Friend, Glorious Friend of all.

Never was love so rich as His,
　　Christ is the Friend we need,
Bringing us peace and holy bliss,
　　Christ is the Friend we need.
　　Trust Him now and ever,
　　He of life's the Giver—
Wonderful Friend, Merciful Friend, Glorious Friend of all.

WAKE TO WORK AND SING.

From the warping pangs of sorrow
   Man must wake to work and sing,
Would he, on each dawning morrow,
   To his fellows gladness bring.

Tears of sadness and heart-aching
   May the inborn man refine,
Sinful trammels from him breaking,
   Drawing to the heart divine.

Yet how oft will he, unthinking,
   Barter all life's bliss away ;
Then, in folly madly sinking,
   Die the death of dark dismay.

Life is only worth the living
   When we live true life to gain,
Through that One who's freely giving
   Life to live that knows no wane.

See, athwart Time's flowing river,
   Golden beams stream from above ;
Fadeless, they are glowing ever
   From our Father's smiles of love.

Wake then ! mortal, from all sadness,
   Tears and sighing must be o'er ;
Work and sing, till earth, in gladness
   Vie the fair eternal shore.

THE MINISTER'S AULD GOON.

Oh, my auld goon, my auld goon,
 That I hae worn aft-times,
Had I the po'er I'd sing o' thee
 In hamely Scottish rhymes ;
I'd tell hoo ye hae happ'd me weel
 While I bade a' come hame
To Christ, the Sun o' Righteousness,
 Wha cam' to save frae shame.

Oh, my auld goon, my auld goon,
 I'll cherish ye wi' care,
Ye'll mind me aft hoo 'neath thy faulds
 I've breathed a heartfelt prayer
That God wha kens oor failin's a'
 Wad draw us nearer hame,
An' on the tablets o' ilk heart
 Write His ain holy name.

Oh, my auld goon, my auld goon,
 Wi' me ye've felt time's wear;
An' as to thee, change comes to a',
 We canna aye bide here.
When comes the ca' to young an' auld
 May a' be airted hame
Trough love o' Him, I've ever tauld
 His love is aye the same.

Oh, my auld goon, my auld goon,
   I'll no' hide ye frae view,
Although I ken that leal kind hearts
   Ha'e gi'en me ane that's new.
'Twill mind me o' that land aboon,
   That everlastin' hame,
Where, robed in white 'mid heavenly light,
   We'll meet an' praise His name.

At a soiree held to celebrate the semi-jubilee of the Rev. R. Workman Orr, minister of Bank Street U.P. Church, Brechin, as reported in the *Brechin Advertiser*, Feb. 5th, 1889, in reply to the presentation of a new pulpit gown, he spoke as follows:—" If I were a poet, especially one of these ' Modern Scottish Poets ' of whom our friend Mr Edwards so delightfully tells us, I would certainly write something worthy of the old garment, which, in its own way, has been so helpful to me during fourteen years. Perhaps some one will take the hint, and write for me ' The Sang of the Minister's Auld Goon.' "

At the request of Mr Edwards, the above verses were written.

THE LOST BIT SILLER.

I'll gae soop the flure wi' keen, tentie care,
　　An' I'll keep on't a watchfu' e'e.
Gi'e owre the search ?　Na, never, guidman,
　　Till the lost bit o' siller I see.

We hann'at to spare, let me coont aince mair,
　　Ay, certes, but it isna here ;
Hoo did it fa' frae oot o' my haund ?
　　True its loss makes me feel unco queer.

I'll gae soop the flure wi' still greater care,
　　For gotten that siller maun be.
There its fund at last, baith safe an' soond,
　　An' my puir heart is reemin' wi' glee.

My wishers weel, an' my neibors atweel,
　　Baith eastward an' westward I'll ca',
That they may join in the joy that's mine,
　　Though the lost bit o' siller was sma'.

There's something to lose, an' something to choose,
　　Ken ye ocht, freens, what they may be ?
'Tis the soul that's thine, an' heaven owre a',
　　God has brocht it sae near you an' me.

We maun humbly believe, aye seek an' receive,
　　Frae the God abune a', the gift—
Eternal life—an' tent it wi' care,
　　Else we'll dwellna ayont the blue lift.

AN INFANT'S PRAYER.

'Tis an infant's simple pray'r
Breath'd upon the evening air,
Kneeling at its mother's feet,
Murm'ring in a voice so sweet,
" Gentle Jesus, meek and mild,
Look upon a little child."

Loud through heaven though anthems ring
Praise to our eternal King,
Who will doubt the Saviour dear
Lowly bends the words to hear—
" Pity my simplicity,
Suffer me to come to Thee."

He who reigns supreme above
Full of tenderness and love,
Will to answer this request,
Give the blessings He thinks best.

May we who life's pathway roam
Like the children trusting come,
Lowly bending at His feet,
Ask that life be made complete.

Love and mercy His to give,
Ours the joy in Him to live,
And as closes each spent day
Simply like the children pray—
" Gentle Jesus, meek and mild,
Keep and lead a trusting child."